The Staircase

Rena Cooper

Copyright © 2021 Rena Cooper

The moral right of the author has been asserted.

Apart from any fair dealing for the purposes of research or private study, or criticism or review, as permitted under the Copyright, Designs and Patents Act 1988, this publication may only be reproduced, stored or transmitted, in any form or by any means, with the prior permission in writing of the publishers, or in the case of reprographic reproduction in accordance with the terms of licences issued by the Copyright Licensing Agency. Enquiries concerning reproduction outside those terms should be sent to the publishers.

Matador
9 Priory Business Park,
Wistow Road, Kibworth Beauchamp,
Leicestershire. LE8 0RX
Tel: 0116 279 2299
Email: books@troubador.co.uk
Web: www.troubador.co.uk/matador
Twitter: @matadorbooks

ISBN 978 1800465 169

British Library Cataloguing in Publication Data.
A catalogue record for this book is available from the British Library.

Printed and bound in Great Britain by 4edge Limited
Typeset in 11pt Minion Pro by Troubador Publishing Ltd, Leicester, UK

Matador is an imprint of Troubador Publishing Ltd

In loving memory of my parents,
Nell and Frank Murgatroyd,
who got it right more often than they ever knew.

Contents

Chapter 1. Edward 1

Chapter 2. James 12

Chapter 3. The Plan 22

Chapter 4. Missing 37

Chapter 5. A Voyage 49

Chapter 6. The Wild Goose Chase 61

Chapter 7. Bicycles and Buses 74

Chapter 8. Seal Island 89

Chapter 9. A Rescue 102

Chapter 10. People and Plans 116

Chapter 11. Rosemary and Others 129

Chapter 1

Edward

He would always remember the staircase. He knew that, even if he lived to be very old, he would always remember it just as it was today. It would come to him when he slept and whenever he walked through an avenue of trees or heard someone in the distance playing the piano.

Mapledene Avenue was in a faded part of the town that had seen better days. The terraces of tall town houses stretched along both sides of the tree-lined street until about half way, where one side of the avenue was occupied not by houses but by a large red-brick school surrounded by mature trees, manicured lawns and playing fields that seemed to stretch forever. By late afternoon, the grounds were busy and noisy with football and rugby teams making the most of the end of the day. The shouts of the eager boys and their cheering friends rang out loud and clear on the summer air. They were the lucky ones. They had no knowledge of the staircase. Edward, however, was all too familiar with every step.

There were six flights and seventy-two steps in all, not counting the two outside the front door. There was also another staircase, a flight of stone steps that led from the hallway down to the basement below. These steps led to the kitchen. He'd been down there once but he preferred not to think about that.

On the ground floor, he was welcomed by Mrs Lockie. She was kind to him, said how pleased she was to see him, asked about his mother and generally made a great fuss. Probably, she understood, felt sorry for him, knew that he didn't want to be there, wanted to run as fast as his legs would carry him in the opposite direction. However, she would smile, take his jacket, hang it up on the hallstand and wait for him while he sat on the bottom step to take off his outdoor shoes and put on the slippers his mother insisted on packing into his case. Once he was on his way, she would wish him good luck and head off down the stone steps into the kitchen. It was the same every time. It was always the same.

This Friday evening began like every other Friday evening. Edward left his father at the gate of 145, Mapledene Avenue, just as usual, and rang the bell in the porch, just as he always did. His father never ventured beyond the gate but always waited until Edward was safely inside the house. Probably making sure he didn't make a run for it!

Mrs Lockie was there to open the door for him just as she always did, ushering him into the depths of the hallway. The entrance hall was gloomy, with embossed green wallpaper and carpets that looked as if, like the avenue itself, they had seen better days; the furniture, what there was of it, was of dark wood and, immediately behind the front door, was the tall carved hallstand that was usually laden with coats and jackets by the time Edward got there.

Once on the staircase, Edward wasted no time. Each of the three floors above was reached by two flights of stairs that were broken by a small landing at the point where the staircase folded back on itself. The dark wallpaper continued all the way up to the top, as did the threadbare carpet in the form of a maroon patterned runner, held in place by dark wooden stair rods. The ceiling was far above. Looking for it made you feel dizzy. The wide bannisters were highly polished and smelled of lavender but Edward kept well away from them because the further up he climbed the more terrifying became the view through the iron railings that were the only things between himself and the yawning depths of the stairwell. Edward had no head for heights.

The staircase was dimly lit and filled with shadows, like the rest of the house, but the landings were softened a little by the addition of octagonal mahogany tables. There was one of these on each landing. On each one, Mrs Lockie had carefully positioned ornate Chinese vases of varying sizes filled with faded silk flowers and tall, arching peacock feathers. On each table there was a lamp. These were always lit, their dusty shades, long-since faded of all colour, allowing only the palest of light to guide those who made their weary way towards the upper rooms. As the sun never reached the inner depths of this house, the air was cool and there was a pervading smell of damp and the passage of time; the lamps and the flowers, like the carpets and everything else about this house, had remained unchanged during Edward's two years as a weekly visitor. It was as if it were frozen in time, a time that had long since passed.

It was, however, the first floor that presented the greatest challenge. At this point, Edward always tried to move quickly and quietly. It was here that he was most likely to encounter Mr Lockie. Today, he was out of luck. The door to the salon at the front of the house flew open as he reached it and the overpowering figure of Mr Lockie emerged. A tall, thin man, he was dressed in the light grey suit that he always wore but, on this occasion, he was also sporting a vivid red-spotted bow tie that made Edward think of a circus clown. He was afraid of circus clowns – and he was afraid of Mr Lockie!

"My dear boy, how are you?" Mr Lockie always called him 'dear boy'. "We haven't had a chat for ages but I'm going to put that right as soon as I can. Now, tell me, how are you getting on?"

Edward mumbled something about everything being fine and then added something else about being late so that he would be able to keep moving in the direction of the stairs to the floor above. As he passed close to Mr Lockie, he was sure he could smell whisky or something like it on his breath. He was also holding a smouldering cigar in his left hand; the smell of smoke mingled with the stale air on the landing. It made Edward feel sick.

Reaching the next floor was always a relief although, for his own reasons, he wasted no time in leaving it far below him. Today was a good day. All was quiet. The last two flights were soon behind him and Edward finally stopped in front of the door of the salon at the very back of the house. He knocked once and immediately heard Miss Gilpin calling to him to come in. There was no going back now. There never was.

The room, which was more like a garret at the very top of the house, was even darker than the stairwell except for the pool of light that illuminated Miss Gilpin's smiling summer face. Outside, the seasons came and went but in this house it was always winter.

"Hello, Edward! Good to see you! I hope you've had an interesting week and done lots of practising for me."

Edward hadn't had a particularly interesting week but there had been a good deal of practising. His father had seen to that. "I've put my name down for the under-thirteens football club," he replied. "I probably won't get into the team. I'm not much good. I'm only doing it to please James. He's a really good footballer."

Miss Gilpin nodded her approval. "It'll do you good, Edward. I'm sure you'll enjoy it. I hope you get into the team." She swung round to open the window immediately behind her; a ripple of warm air rattled the blind and made the heavy curtains move. "There, that's better," said Miss Gilpin, turning back towards the grand piano that dominated the room. "Now we can breathe."

Miss Gilpin was the only good thing about Mapledene Avenue, the only good thing about The Lockie School of Music. She knew what Edward knew, namely that he would never ever learn to play the piano. He would never ever learn to play the piano even if he practised and practised non-stop for a million years. She knew, as he did, that it was quite hopeless, a waste of his parents' money and Miss Gilpin's valuable time but neither of them mentioned that. Every week, they struggled through the hour long lesson, with his dedicated teacher being as encouraging as anyone could be, while Edward stumbled through his pieces, making the same old mistakes he'd made the week before and the week before that. In all probability, he'd be making them the following week as well.

After half an hour, they always stopped for a five minute break. That was usually the best bit of the lesson. However, for once, it proved to be otherwise. Normally, whatever the time of year, they would take a moment or two to gaze out of the window into the topmost branches of the beech tree in the garden. It stretched skywards almost as tall as the house itself; casting your eyes downward to peer through the branches towards the ground far below was a tingling sensation. The tree was vast, its vibrant colours changing with the seasons while the garden, far, far below, lay hidden beneath its dappled shade or, in autumn, buried deep under piles of red and golden leaves. Edward liked looking down through the branches of the beech tree, even though he usually avoided heights, but, on this occasion, as the window was open, he was keeping his distance. It was a long way down.

Miss Gilpin didn't look at the tree. She looked at Edward. "I have some news for you, Edward," she said. "Very soon, in about a month, I'm getting married." She held out her left hand to show him the ring on her fourth finger. He hadn't noticed it before but now he could see it sparkling in the light from the window. Miss Gilpin continued. "We get on very well, you and I, so I am very sorry to say that I will be leaving as Mr Lockie is not keen on married ladies continuing in work. It's a bit old-fashioned these days but there it is! It's one of his rules, I'm afraid. Still, we do have a few more weeks together and then Mr Lockie is going to take on all my pupils himself until he finds a new teacher to take my place. You'll be with the top man, the maestro himself, so we'll have to work really hard to polish up all your pieces before the big day comes around. Don't worry! Mr Lockie is a very good teacher. You'll be fine."

Edward knew – and suspected that Miss Gilpin also knew – that he would be anything but fine! She looked happy and sad all at the same time. Edward tried to look pleased. He wasn't quite sure what was the right thing to say on such an occasion but, in the end, he just smiled and told her that he would let his mum know all about it and explain to his father that he would be getting a new teacher.

The second half of the lesson dragged on until, finally, it was time to go. Miss Gilpin filled in his homework notebook, just as she always did, and gave him some words of encouragement. As he was leaving, he paused briefly before opening the door to the hallway and turned his head for just long enough to take one last look at Miss Gilpin. She had her back towards him as she was closing the window again, but he thought he heard her start to say something. Still, by the time she'd turned round to say it, he was already on his way down the stairs.

On his way to the floor below, he met Rosemary on her way up. Rosemary was younger than Edward and quite new to The Lockie School of Music, but it was obvious that she was going to be a star pupil. She'd played at the Christmas concert, after only a few lessons, and had been faultless in front of an audience of proud parents gathered in Mr Lockie's upstairs salon for this harrowing annual occasion. All Miss Gilpin's pupils were performing that day, including Edward. He'd had nightmares about it for weeks beforehand. In the end, he'd managed to get through his pieces without making too many mistakes, but he'd known from his father's face that he'd failed to impress.

All the mums and dads had clapped, including his own mum. She'd smiled and looked genuinely pleased, but he'd known that he hadn't been good enough. His father hadn't spoken a word to him all the way home on the bus. His mum had kept telling him how proud she'd been, but it was no good. He'd been a disappointment.

Rosemary looked happy, as she always did. Her weekly lesson followed Edward's so they often passed on the stairs. She smiled and spoke to him, but he didn't stop to reply. He kept on going and he didn't pause when he reached the floor below – but then he never did linger there. On that floor, there were two salons where the senior pupils had their lessons. The music hurt Edward's ears.

Mr Lockie was nowhere to be seen, which was a huge relief, and Edward reached the ground floor in good time. Mrs Lockie was waiting for him. "How did you get on today?" she asked. She always asked him the same thing.

"Fine, thank you," Edward replied politely. Like Mrs Lockie, he always said precisely the same thing. It was a ritual. Next, Mrs Lockie helped him on with his jacket, watched him pack away his slippers and waited patiently while he put on his outdoor shoes. Last of all, she produced a tin of sweets. That was a surprise! Edward helped himself to a chocolate caramel in gold foil and put it into his pocket to eat on the bus going home. "Thank you very much," he said, picking up his music case and heading for the front door. Almost there!

"See you next Friday, Edward," Mrs Lockie called as he headed off down the path to meet his father. Edward turned to smile but said nothing. He wasn't quite sure what he was going to do – not yet – but, in his mind, he was clear about one very important thing. One way or another, he was going to put a stop to The Lockie School of Music forever!

The walk to the bus was a silent affair. His father was carrying a neatly folded newspaper and a copy of *The Eagle*, reading material for the journey home. At the bus stop, his father took the music case from Edward's hand and opened it in order to retrieve the homework notebook. Miss Gilpin always jotted down a few comments about Edward's progress and listed what he was to practise during the week ahead.

Not a word was spoken. His father read without comment then replaced the notebook in the case, which he handed back to Edward. Another ritual had been completed. Thankfully, their bus arrived almost immediately. Sometimes, in winter, it was freezing at the bus stop, but tonight the evening was warm and there were very few people about. Once on the bus, they went straight upstairs. Edward hated upstairs on the bus; he always felt sick on the journey to his music lesson but, for some reason, despite being on the top deck, he never felt ill on the way home. However, the atmosphere upstairs on the double-decker was always thick with smoke and the smell of stale tobacco. Edward hated it. The strong smell seemed to cling to your hair and your clothes for a long time afterwards but, nevertheless, they always had to go up the stairs to sit on the top deck, whether he liked it or not, so that his father could smoke his cigarettes; smoking was not allowed downstairs.

On the homeward journey, Edward did his best to make the chocolate caramel last for as long as possible, while he pretended to read *The Eagle*. He thought hard about The Lockie School of Music and how much he wanted never to see it again. He would be sorry not to see Miss Gilpin, but she would be leaving some day soon and so that was that. Mrs Lockie was kind. However, he remembered, with horror, the ordeal of the Christmas Party Tea for all the young pianists. She'd held it after the annual concert. It was a 'tradition'. While all the parents enjoyed afternoon tea in the upstairs salon and listened to Mr Lockie giving a recital, the pupils, after a final round of applause, had been escorted down to the basement kitchen for a buffet, prepared by Mrs Lockie herself.

The feast had been set out on a large, round wooden table: cakes, sandwiches, biscuits, jellies. Edward had never seen such a spread in all his life. Neither had he ever seen a food fight before. Most of the pupils who went to Mr Lockie's rather expensive music school came from families that Edward's mum described as being 'well-to-do' and attended private schools in the city, while Edward went to the local primary near his home and lived in a small, rented council house. His parents, however, were very strong on manners and remembering your 'Ps and Qs'. No one at Mrs Lockie's kitchen table that afternoon had seemed the least bit interested in remembering their manners or their 'Ps and Qs' and, although not a particularly nervous boy, Edward had been relieved when the exhausted hostess had finally announced that it was time to go back upstairs and join the mums and dads once more. Edward had had nightmares about that day for weeks afterwards. One way and another, he'd had lots of nightmares about The Lockie School of Music – but he was going to put a stop to that.

Edward made himself a silent promise. It was a promise that, one way or another, he was determined to keep. With a sidelong glance towards his father, now engrossed in his copy of *The Evening Post*, he vowed that, whatever happened, he would never again climb that staircase. He would never again sit on the top deck of a bus and never again, in his whole life, would he attempt to play a piano!

Chapter 2

James

James loved Fridays. The football club met after school and then, when he got home, he knew *The Wizard* and *The Eagle* would be waiting. Also, he and his mum and dad nearly always had fish and chips from the shop on Friday evenings. It was the best day of the week by a mile. Also, at the weekend, he could look forward to spending more time with Edward, who was his best friend in and out of school. This week, he'd managed to persuade Edward to join the football club. Up until now, Edward hadn't been able to come along on Fridays as he'd had to go somewhere with his dad every week straight after school. However, training nights were now going to be held on Wednesdays, with matches at weekends, so that would work out much better. He felt sure that Edward would fit into the team really well.

James and his parents lived in a rambling flat over the grocery store that they owned and ran. Their shop, the finest in Craigbank, was the sort that sold things you couldn't find just anywhere. The butter came in special churns all the way from Denmark and the cheeses came from all over the country as well as from Holland and France. Many of the jams and chutneys were made by James's mum, who was an excellent cook, and the free range eggs came from a local farm. The shop was popular with the locals, who liked to come in and catch up on all the news while they were collecting their groceries. The prices were fair and the shop was clean because James's mum and dad worked hard to make sure that everything was just so. They were very proud of their shop, which they had built up from nothing. It was double-fronted so that, inside, it seemed more like two shops, with one half being used as a grocery store while the other half was licensed to sell wines and spirits. James's dad knew quite a lot about wine and sometimes gave talks about it. Every day, the floor was swept and washed clean, with fresh sawdust dusted over it to make sure that no-one slipped, especially if they were carrying an expensive bottle of something good or a jar of home-made jam. The shop always had its own special smell that changed with the seasons. In winter, the warm scent of dried fruit and spices told everyone that Christmas was on its way. Now, in summer, it smelled of ripe strawberries from the fruit farm on the loch road.

When he arrived home, James could see that his mum and dad were busy serving customers; his mum was in the grocery, where there was a small queue, and his dad was helping an elderly gentleman to choose some wine. James didn't linger. With a quick wave to let them both know that he was safely home, he shot straight upstairs, just as he always did. Minutes later, he was stretched out on his bed with his copy of *The Wizard*. The flat had two floors and, as it had been a sunny day, the upstairs rooms were warm. The window was wide open. Outside, the summer air was still. In a few days, it would be the school holidays. Life was good!

It wasn't until he heard his mum calling for him that James realised he'd fallen asleep.

"Come on down!" she called up from the kitchen. "Fish and chips, nice and hot on the table! Wash your hands and get yourself down here or we'll have to eat yours as well! Come on, James!" He didn't have to be told twice.

It was when they were clearing the table after supper that Mrs McLintock brought up the subject of Edward and Friday afternoons. "Has Edward told you where he goes on Fridays, yet?" she asked. "I know you've been wondering what the mystery is all about."

James shook his head and reached for the tea towel. He usually helped with the washing-up on Fridays. Fridays were pocket money nights.

"Well, I think I may be able to help you there, but you mustn't say anything to Edward. He must have his own reasons for saying nothing about it at school."

James waited expectantly. His mum was very good at finding things out and just as good at keeping secrets. She'd begun to wash the plates and he was ready to dry them. "Edward is learning to play the piano. He goes up to the city on the bus with his father for his lesson every Friday. He's been going there for about two years."

It took a few moments for the words to sink in. James just stared at his mum in disbelief, the tea towel unused. "But Edward isn't a bit musical," he said. "Edward just moves his lips in Music at school and pretends to be singing. He doesn't actually sing a note and he never even sings in Assembly! He doesn't even sing carols at Christmas!"

It was true. Edward was pretty good at most things. He and James were always at the top of the class. Music, however, was definitely not his strong point. It just didn't make any sense at all and James didn't hesitate to say so.

"Well," his mum continued, "Mrs Cuthbertson has been scrubbing floors all over the town and working long hours in the laundry so that they could buy a piano for Edward and pay for him to have lessons and, on top of that, he goes to one of the most expensive music schools in the city. What do you think of that?"

James put down the plate that, by now, he'd dried several times. "I don't know yet, but I won't say anything to anyone," he said, "and I won't tell Edward that I know. Maybe he's waiting until he's really good at it before he tells anyone so that it will be a big surprise. Mr Cuthbertson can play lots of different instruments. He's really good. Perhaps Edward is going to be like his dad."

His mum gave James what could only be described as an old-fashioned look, but she didn't say any more. She wondered if she'd actually said a bit too much.

Later, back in his room, James thought hard about what his mother had told him. There were things he knew that she didn't and, like his mum, James was very good at keeping secrets. He'd thought about telling her several times but, somehow, the words always got stuck. Anyway, he'd promised Edward and a promise is a promise.

At Lomond Street Primary, James and Edward were in the top class, ready to move on to secondary school after the holidays. They'd both done very well in all the leaving exams and so they would be going up to Craigallen High School in August; with luck, they would be together in the same class. Their teacher, Mr Hogg, had given them excellent end-of-term reports and told them how pleased he was with their work and yet Edward hadn't seemed happy, not really. When James had asked him what was wrong, he'd just shrugged his shoulders and talked about something else, but James thought that he could make a reasonably good guess at what the problem might be. However, now that he knew about the music lessons, he was even more worried. It might be time to ask Edward about it again, but he couldn't let him know that he knew about the piano. He was pretty sure he wasn't worried about school. School was good and they had Mr Hogg, the deputy head, who was great and good at football. He'd once played for a local club.

Mr Hogg was a hard task-master. Every Friday morning, there was the weekly test in English and Maths. By the following Monday morning, Mr Hogg had marked all forty papers and was ready with the results. Everyone had to be prepared for The Big Move. The class was set out in four rows of double desks, with folding flap seats, a bit like the ones in the cinema, except that the ones in The Regal had cushions. The desks were pretty ancient, but the strong, metal frames showed no signs that they were anywhere near being scrapped. They were probably destined to be around for decades to come. Many of the desk lids bore carvings left by previous occupants of Room Seven and some of the pupils swore blind they'd found the initials of their own parents, who'd passed that way many years before. It was not impossible!

Every Monday morning, they all had to get their possessions together so that the class could be reseated in order of their test marks. It was a weekly ritual that held little fear for James and Edward as they were always at the top of the class and never had to suffer the embarrassment of being moved down. Sometimes James was first and Edward second; sometimes it was the other way around. It was hard on some of the others and sometimes there were tears. Mr Hogg would say, "Well, no good crying. You'll just have to work harder next week!" James felt sorry for those who had to move down or, even worse, move to the second or third rows. The ones in the fourth row, by the windows, he didn't worry about at all. They were so used to being there that they actually didn't seem to care any more. They'd given up, resigned themselves to their fate! At least they could look out of the windows until it was time to go to Carson Street Secondary. That was where all those who failed the final exam had to go. It was in the roughest part of the town and had bars at some of the windows. James and Edward always hurried past it when they went into town.

James was looking out of the window now, the window of his own room that looked out on to the yard at the back of the shop. That was where his mum hung out the weekly wash and where his dad stored stock in a large outhouse that took up almost half of the whole area. There was still room for a few pot plants and a small table and chairs for eating outside on warmer days. The high, wooden fence and gate at the back meant that they could be private and the delivery lane beyond was fairly quiet, but James wished they had a garden with lots of grass for playing football. Still, there was always The Reccy, the recreation ground about a hundred yards along the road.

That was where he and Edward spent most of every Saturday. That was a very good second best. There was a football field, a running track, tennis courts, parallel bars and a large, white pavilion that was used only on special occasions like tournaments or match days. Edward was a fast runner so he loved the track. He was hoping to join The Craigbank Harriers when he was a bit older. James thought that Edward's speed would be helpful to the football team. They needed someone who could really move. James was usually in goal. He liked that best.

Through in the sitting room, James could now hear his parents settling down to watch television. They liked to relax in the evenings and put their feet up after standing all day in the shop. James could hear an announcer's voice introducing some programme, but he couldn't make out what it was. Later, he would wander through to have a look at what was on but, for the moment, he was content to read his comics. However, it was difficult to concentrate because he couldn't stop thinking about Edward and the piano. Why hadn't he told him? Why hadn't he mentioned it?

After only a few minutes, James put *The Wizard* to one side. It was no use. He couldn't concentrate. All he could think about was that day, a few months ago, when he'd gone to collect Edward to go to the track. He'd been a bit early that Saturday morning as the sun had been really bright and had wakened him long before his usual time. He'd had his breakfast earlier and headed off straight away so that they could get there before The Reccy got too busy. Edward was always keen and ready with his kit bag all packed so James had known for sure that he'd be pleased to see him.

As usual, he'd gone straight round to the back door, where he'd knocked three times. No-one had answered so he'd peered through the kitchen window. No-one was to be seen. The absence of Mrs Cuthbertson's bike, which always stood by the fence, had told him that she'd probably left for one of her cleaning jobs or gone shopping a bit earlier than usual. James had opened the back door a little and called Edward's name. There had been no response so he'd let himself in, just as he'd done many times before. Then, he'd stopped dead in his tracks.

The house was a small council house on the edge of a large estate; the inner kitchen door opened into a long hallway. At the far end was the front door, which was just beyond the staircase that led up to the bedrooms. Mr Cuthbertson, a tall, sinewy man, had been standing in the hallway. Edward had been pressed up against the wall, his father gripping him tightly by his right arm and, as James had watched in horror from the kitchen doorway, he'd seen Mr Cuthbertson strike Edward several times. The man had clearly lost his temper. Edward was vainly trying to protect himself with his left arm by holding it up in front of his face, while trying desperately to break free from his father's grip.

At first, neither of them had realised that James was standing in the doorway, that he could see all that was happening. James had stood rooted to the spot, unable to believe what was before his eyes. All at once, a blow to Edward's head had sent him reeling into the opposite wall. There had been a dull thud as he'd hit the woodwork – the wooden panelling of the staircase – and then he'd crumpled in a heap on the floor.

As Edward's father had raised his hand once again, James had found his voice. "No!" he'd shouted. "Please, Mr Cuthbertson, please don't hit him again! Please don't hit Edward any more!"

Instinctively, he'd stepped forward to place himself between father and son. He'd faced up to Edward's father, seen the anger in his face, waited for him to strike the next blow, waited for what seemed like forever, before he'd realised that it was over. The man had looked down at Edward, who was slowly rising to his feet. Mr Cuthbertson's eyes had shifted from one boy to the other and then he'd stared down at his hands as if he couldn't quite believe what he'd done. Without another word, he'd disappeared into the living room at the front of the house and closed the door behind him.

In the silence that had followed, Edward had said nothing. He'd simply picked up his kit bag from behind the kitchen door and signalled to James that they needed to go. It was obvious that he'd been hurt and that he'd been crying but, as they'd walked to The Reccy, Edward had used his handkerchief to dry his tear-stained face, had pulled up his running socks and drawn his jerkin around his shoulders as if to comfort himself. He'd spoken not a word nor made any attempt to explain what James had seen but, as they'd approached the playing fields, he'd made him promise never to tell anyone about it.

By the time they'd reached the track, it had become clear to James that Edward had no intention of explaining what had happened. It had been just as obvious that he would not be mentioning it ever again.

From that day on, whenever they were changing for Games, James had kept an eye on Edward as they got into their kit. Once, he'd noticed a purple bruise on his left arm but, when he asked him about it, Edward had simply said that he'd fallen out of a tree. James had felt uneasy about that explanation as Edward was nervous of heights. He'd never been known to climb trees.

Now, stretched out on his bed, James was deep in thought. How he wished he hadn't made that promise to keep quiet! Now that he knew about the piano lessons, he couldn't help feeling that, somehow, Fridays might very well have something to do with what he'd seen on that dreadful day. It was a cold feeling in the pit of his stomach as if something bad were just around the corner – and it was a feeling that just wouldn't go away.

Chapter 3

The Plan

On Saturday, James and Edward met, as usual, at The Reccy. James almost forgot about his worries as Edward was on good form, beating his own personal best around the cinder track and performing a new routine on the parallel bars. Despite the warm weather, the playing fields were quiet and they pretty much had the place to themselves for most of the morning. They sat on the pavilion steps to eat their sandwiches and then, in the afternoon, when the others arrived for the football matches, they decided to join in with a game of five-a-side. Edward looked as if he was really enjoying himself. Hadn't a care in the world. No need to worry, after all. James was relieved. No-one mentioned piano lessons.

On Sunday, Edward was going to be helping his mum

with jobs. At least, that was what he said to James, who was disappointed not to be going fishing in the Craigie Burn. They nearly always went there on Sundays even if it was raining but, although they did their best, they hardly ever caught anything. Still, it was good for a laugh and they usually bumped into some of the men from the angling club. They were good fun and James and Edward liked listening to their stories and inspecting all the amazing fishing tackle that the old boys had collected over the years. James thought about going down to the burn on his own but, in the end, he cleaned and oiled his bike and finished up kicking an old tennis ball about in the back yard. School would be finishing on Wednesday so there would be the whole summer holiday to go fishing and do whatever they wanted.

The last three days of school were the usual end-of-year ritual with everyone collecting their artwork, being cheered for any prizes they'd won and helping Mr Hogg to tidy up the classroom for a party on the last day. Mr Hogg gave everyone a pep-talk about working hard at secondary school and being a credit to Lomond Street Primary when they moved on in August. It was a bit sad really and James was glad when it was all over. He'd enjoyed being in Mr Hogg's class and so had Edward; they both made a point of thanking him for everything before they left on the final day. Mr Hogg looked a bit embarrassed and said how much he'd enjoyed having them in his class. He told them that he hoped they'd come back some time and tell him how they were doing at Craigallen. They both said they would, but James had a feeling that it would never happen, and he also had the feeling that Edward and Mr Hogg were thinking the same thing! It was just the sort of thing that people said to take the edge off saying 'good-bye'.

On Wednesday, after school closed for the summer holidays, Edward had tea at James's house. He always did. Mrs McLintock made a special celebration spread, which was very much appreciated. It made up for all the fuss at school. Everything was just as normal. Nothing different. By request, sausage, egg and chips, followed by all the ice-cream you could eat! Excellent!

It was when Edward was getting ready for home that he broke the news that he wouldn't be coming over the next day. He said that he'd promised to help his mum with some jobs in the garden. James didn't know what to make of that. For a start, they always went fishing on the first day of the holidays and, secondly, Edward's mum wasn't really into gardening as their garden was the size of a postage stamp and mainly down to grass. Edward went on to say that he would be going to town with his dad on Friday so he'd have to leave meeting up until after that and then they could start to make their plans for the rest of the holidays.

James began to feel uneasy. Something was wrong. Something was very wrong! After thanking Mrs McLintock for his tea, Edward gathered his things together and set off for home. James watched as he walked off along the pavement and paused at the traffic lights. As a rule, Edward would stop at the junction and turn round to wave back at James before crossing to the other side of the main road. For once, he didn't look back. He just kept on going, his school bag slung over his left shoulder and his folder of artwork tucked firmly under his right arm. There were quite a few people about so Edward was soon lost in the crowd. James closed the door and went inside.

Mrs McLintock was clearing away the tea things when James told her all about it. His mum thought hard for a moment and then she shrugged her shoulders. "Perhaps he is going to help in the garden. Perhaps he's going to cut the grass or sweep the paths or something," she said. "As for Friday, well, I suspect that he's going to have to go for that piano lesson and doesn't want to say so. Not quite ready to tell anyone about that. Try not to worry about it. He'll tell you in his own good time." When she saw James's crestfallen expression, she put an arm around his shoulders. "You've got all the holidays to go fishing or do whatever you want, so cheer up. You can use your spare time to help your dad give the outhouse a good sort out. It certainly needs it and, you never know, there could be some extra pocket money around if you play your cards right and do a good job!" James wasn't exactly cheered up by this suggestion but, as he was saving up for a new fishing rod, he wasn't about to look a gift horse in the mouth. Some extra pocket money could come in handy.

Thursday was spent earning the extra pocket money, as agreed. Digging out the outhouse was a dirty job that took most of the day, but the storeroom looked good at the end of it and James's dad was pleased. Friday, however, seemed to drag. The weather was warm and the sun shone all day. At a loose end, James spent the morning tidying his bedroom and cleaning his football boots. In the afternoon, he wandered along to The Reccy to see if there was a match going on. There was. He knew most of the kids in one of the teams and, as none of them wanted to be in goal, he was able to join in. Several asked about Edward, but James just told them that he was helping his mum. During the match, he had to keep his mind on the game. He stopped three good attempts at goal but failed to save a penalty. Still, his team managed to settle for a one-all draw and everyone went home reasonably happy. However, it was as he was making his own way home that James began to feel uneasy once again. He thought of going up to Edward's house to see if he was in but decided against it. Tomorrow was Saturday and Edward would probably be round first thing in the morning to see if he wanted to go fishing. Best leave things alone!

Edward was not in the habit of keeping secrets from James but he knew that, for once, he had no choice. There was no guarantee that his plan would work but, for now, it was best that no-one knew anything about it. James, in particular, must know absolutely nothing about it. If questions were asked, and they would be asked, it was best that James wouldn't have to lie. It was necessary for him not to have any of the answers. Edward had been doing a great deal of thinking since his last visit to The Lockie School of Music. He knew now exactly what he needed to do. Every detail had been considered. Every eventuality. Cautious by nature, he knew the risks he would be taking, but there could be no going back now.

Thursday was spent making preparations. His mum was working at the laundry most of that day and his father was taking his piano accordion into the city. He had a pitch near the railway station and could usually make good money busking there. The police enjoyed the music, even made requests for particular tunes, so they were more than happy to turn a blind eye. They never moved him on. In the evening, he would be playing in the pub by the riverside. He didn't make quite so much money there because he spent half of his takings on whisky, but it kept him out until late, which would give Edward plenty of time to himself. He'd been told to use that day for practising his exam pieces but he had other plans. He would need that time for preparation. He would have his supper early, with his mum, and then head up to his own room before his father's return. No matter how late it was, his dad would be ready for some supper. Edward intended to be in bed by then.

When it was time to say goodnight to his mum, she was already getting ready for the arrival of her husband. The kitchen table was set and she was warming the oven to heat up a mutton pie that she'd bought on her way home from work. Pie and beans tonight! Comfort food! Edward put his arms around his mum and hugged her as hard as he could.

"Hey!" she cried. "I don't usually get all this attention. You're breaking my bones. What have I done to deserve this?"

Edward didn't answer. He just gave her a pretend salute and headed for the hallway.

As he was going up the stairs, his mum called after him, "Edward, have you got everything ready for your lesson tomorrow? Your dad will be sure to ask when he gets in. You know what he's like."

Edward didn't hesitate. "Yes. Don't worry, Mum. I've got everything ready," he called as he reached his bedroom door. And he had!

Friday was very quiet as his mum and dad were out for most of the day. His mum was working at two of her cleaning jobs and his dad was providing entertainment at the bowling club by playing the piano for a wedding party. There was, of course, no school for Edward, so that gave him some more valuable time to himself, which was useful. As the afternoon wore on, his father returned in good time for their usual trip into the city. Edward was waiting for him with his case in his hand.

The bus ride to The Lockie School of Music passed uneventfully except that, for the first time ever, Edward didn't feel travel sick. His mind was busy and he felt sure that his heart was beating so loudly that his father, in the seat next to him, would be able to hear it. They walked in silence along Mapledene Avenue, just as usual, with Edward clutching his music case in his left hand, as he always did. When they arrived at the gateway, his father stepped back to let him go through and then he waited on the pavement, as always, to make sure that the door was opened before he went on his way. He never made any attempt to speak to Mrs Lockie, who opened the door and ushered Edward inside. Edward knew that, as soon as the door closed behind them, his father would head for the cafe on the corner. He always did.

Once in the hallway, after the usual words of welcome, Mrs Lockie waited for Edward to change into his slippers but, for once, received an apology.

"I'm very sorry, Mrs Lockie," explained Edward. "I've forgotten my slippers today. Do you mind if I just wipe my feet on the mat?"

She smiled. "Not at all, my dear," she replied. "You're the only one who ever bothers to bring slippers. Mostly, they all charge up the stairs, mud and all. It's a good job the carpet's an old one. Up you go! Don't you worry!"

Edward felt guilty. Mrs Lockie was kind. It wasn't her fault. None of it was her fault. She was always welcoming and really nice to him. She was nice to everyone, even the hooligans who'd organised the food fight that terrible day. He thought that it was a bit of a shame that he'd never see her again.

He climbed the first half of the staircase that led to the first floor, pausing on the half-landing to look back. Mrs Lockie was just checking to make sure that she'd closed the front door properly. He took a few more steps round the bend in the staircase to make quite sure that he was out of sight from the hallway below, waiting just long enough to hear her feet tip-tapping on the stone stairs as Mrs Lockie made her way back down to the kitchen. It was what she always did. Edward had depended on that. He made no attempt to climb any further. There was no time to lose now. He could hear the sound of marching tunes drifting down from the upper salons. That was an unexpected bonus. The sound of the front door opening and closing would be completely drowned out by the loud military music.

Edward needn't have worried. The front door opened easily and he closed it softly behind him. From the shelter of the porch, he peered towards the gate that opened on to Mapledene Avenue. His father was nowhere to be seen. He checked again before venturing down the tiled path. The avenue appeared to be deserted apart from an elderly man, who was working in his garden further down on the opposite side. As he stepped out on to Mapledene Avenue, Edward looked to his right. He could now just make out his father's retreating figure heading for the main road and the cafe, where he would wait just long enough to have a cup of tea and a sausage roll, before moving on to the newsagents to collect his paper and Edward's comic. He looked very small and far away. Taking care to close the gate as quietly as possible, all the time holding tightly to his music case, Edward turned left along the avenue and began to run.

Edward had always been good at running. That was one of the reasons that James was keen for him to join the football team, but Edward wasn't sure that he was going to live up to expectations. Still, at this moment, speed was all that was necessary. Time was short. For his plan to work, he had to keep up a good pace and that was exactly what he intended to do.

As he drew level with the school playing fields on the opposite side of the avenue, he was surprised to see that the double gates were wide open. He'd assumed that the school would be closed for the summer holidays, but there were lots of people milling about on the rugby pitch to the left. Clearly, some kind of sports event was in full flow, with lots of excitement and noise. In the distance, he could see that one boy was being held shoulder high and carried round the edge of the pitch. Everyone was clapping and cheering. A victorious team captain, perhaps?

Under a large tree, close to the main gate, Edward could see a huge pile of school satchels thrown in a random heap, presumably left there until the end of play or whatever was going on. That was not what stopped him in his tracks. Abandoned by the gateway were several expensive-looking bicycles! Edward had outgrown his own bicycle and his father was adamant that there would be no replacement until he'd passed his grade three music exams. It was obvious to Edward that there was very little chance that he would pass grade two, so grade three was never going to happen. He'd resigned himself to the fact that the only cycling he would be doing would be limited to borrowing James's bike from time to time.

One particularly smart bicycle caught his eye. Behind the saddle, it had a metal rack with a clip attached to it, presumably for holding the owner's schoolbag. Edward hesitated but not for long. It was a stroke of luck that was too good to ignore. He only needed it for fifteen minutes at the most. Not stealing, just borrowing. No one would notice; all eyes were on the hero of the hour!

With his music case hastily clipped in place behind him, Edward pedalled as hard as he could. Not far to go now. This was much easier than running. A stroke of luck!

The avenue was long but there were few people about and no traffic to speak of. He was hot in his woollen jumper, but he was going to need that later on. A quick look over his shoulder reassured him that no one was in pursuit. Keep going! Soon be there! A glance at his watch told him that he was making good time. He was ahead of schedule by the time he reached the Art Gallery and Museum, which marked the end of the avenue. Here, at a busy junction, Mapledene Avenue joined the main road that travelled northwards out of the city. Edward dismounted and cut through the grounds behind the enormous sandstone building that dominated the site. In the car park, there were several rows of racks, which were reserved for bicycles, and that was where Edward parted company with his transport. With luck, someone would find it and return it to its owner.

Removing his jumper, which was too heavy for the warm, summer afternoon, he tied it around his waist and hurried across the busy road, heading for the bus stop. He kept a firm grip on his case. He was going to need that. By his reckoning, he was now about ten minutes ahead of schedule. The queue, however, was already forming and he joined on at the end. There were only half a dozen people in front of him. He'd made it. So far, so good! While he waited, he kept a wary eye on the junction, but there was no sign of his father in pursuit. By now, his absence must have been noticed by Miss Gilpin and Mrs Lockie, but his father would not return to collect him until the appointed time, so he would still be unaware that anything was wrong. Time was on his side. His lesson was one whole hour long. By then, with luck, he would be well on his way.

The bus was dead on time and it was half empty so there was no problem finding a seat. Edward sat right at the front, downstairs, nearest to the driver, who was separated from the passengers by a glass screen. No one would bother him there and he could just sit and do absolutely nothing until he reached the terminus. There would be no riding on the top deck and breathing in all the smoke. Not today! He imagined his father riding home on his own, wondering how his son had managed to give him the slip. It made him smile. In fact, it was all he could do to stop himself from laughing out loud. The conductress gave him a funny look when she came for the money for his ticket.

"You a'right, son?" she asked. "Feelin' sick?"

Edward tried to look serious. "No, I'm fine, thanks," he replied, holding out the exact money for his fare. "I'm fine, thank you." And he was!

Sitting on his own and looking out at the passing scenery reminded Edward of the previous trips he'd made along this very route with his mum. He wished she could be with him now. Suddenly, he felt guilty. She was going to be worried about him. Still, that couldn't be helped. It wouldn't be for long. He had a plan for that, too. It would all come right in the end. It had to! No going back now!

Farms and villages flew by until, finally, the coastline came into view. From the window, Edward was able to recognise several landmarks: the power station in the distance, the radio mast, the sugar boat – which was the hull of an upturned cargo vessel that had been abandoned by its owners long ago – and, finally, the pier that stretched out into the sea and told him that his journey was almost at an end. He put on his jumper and made sure that he was ready to get off at the bus station.

"Castle Bay!" shouted the conductress. "End o' the line, folks! Make sure you've got all yer stuff before you get aff. I dinnae want to be runnin' after you lot all the way alang the front!" She was ready, with her ticket machine in her hand, to head for the canteen and a chance to put her feet up.

Keeping a tight grip on his black, leather music case, Edward stood up and got ready to go. Many of the original passengers had travelled all the way from the city, and so he had to wait for a minute or two until everyone had gathered their belongings together before he could climb down on to the pavement. He was in no hurry. There was plenty of time before he had to be on the move again. Until the morning, all he had to do was wait. It was going to be a long night.

The evening was still warm but Edward knew that, as night approached, that would change; the jumper would come into its own later on. Striding along the sea front, he headed straight for the large, wooden pagoda that stood at the far end of the promenade. There were several of these rather grand shelters all along the seafront, but his destination was the very last one in the line. By now, he hoped that it would be empty. Teatime! With luck, everyone would be heading home or going back to their hotels. Even better than that, not only was the pagoda deserted, the ice-cream van was still there in the car park close by. The ice-cream man was just about to finish up for the day, but he was more than happy to serve one more customer. A large cornet! That would keep him from going thirsty until morning. Excellent timing!

"You all on your own, son?" asked the man in the van.

"I'm waiting for a friend," was Edward's hasty reply. "He'll be along any minute."

Another lie! It made him think of James. He felt bad about keeping him in the dark about everything, but it had to be that way. James was part of the plan, a very important part, although he didn't know that yet.

Edward made his way round to the front of the pagoda and sat down on the wooden seat, facing out towards the sea. He ate his ice-cream first and then the sandwiches that he'd prepared that morning, when he'd had the house to himself. He took the copy of *The Eagle* out of his music case and began to read it. He'd saved it. It would help to pass the time. If he kept still and quiet and out of sight, he should be safe enough until morning.

As the evening cooled, he took out the wind-cheater that he'd packed in his case and drew it around him. It was thin but it would have to do. Better than nothing! The case was small but, without the sheets of music, he'd been able to pack quite a few things that would come in handy and then, of course, there was the money. His father hadn't realised that Edward had discovered his hiding place for his earnings, a thick wad of paper money about which he was keeping very quiet! Edward had known about it for a long time and now it was safely tucked away in the music case by his side. He shivered as he imagined the expression there would be on his father's face when he discovered that it was missing. He wondered if he would appreciate what had been left for him in its place. It was there waiting for him, waiting for him at this very moment, tucked away behind the tallboy in the spare bedroom.

At last, it was dark. Edward settled down, as best he could, to wait for the sunrise. On the horizon, he could just make out the lights of a large fishing boat. It appeared to be at anchor. Somewhere, far beyond that horizon, far from Castle Bay, far from The Lockie School of Music and far, far away from his father's permanent disapproval, lay his destination. All he had to do now was get there!

Chapter 4

Missing

Miss Gilpin looked out of the window. She'd enjoyed her three years at The Lockie School of Music. Playing the piano was what she loved most in all the world and passing that love on to her pupils was what she did best. It seemed so unfair that she would have to leave the job she loved simply because she was getting married, but that was the rule here, as in lots of places, and there was nothing she could do about it. All she could hope for was that Mr Lockie would change his mind. She had a feeling that Mrs Lockie was working behind the scenes to make sure that he did just that. Still, for now, she needed to put her worries to one side and concentrate on preparing for the arrival of her next pupil, Edward.

Miss Gilpin felt sorry for Edward. He was such a pleasant boy, and bright too, but he wasn't a pianist, never going to be. She'd tried talking to his father after the concert, but he was determined that his son would learn to play the piano and that was that! Mr Cuthbertson was obviously a talented musician and he desperately wanted his son to follow in his footsteps. Although musical himself, he was, surprisingly, unable to actually read music and so was not up to teaching his son himself. Edward would have to struggle on at The Lockie School of Music. It was going to be a challenge for him when he had to face his weekly lessons with Mr Lockie, who would be a hard task master. It had been obvious from the look on Edward's face when she'd broken the news that he was not looking forward to her departure. She suspected that he was afraid of Mr Lockie although, to his credit, the boy hadn't said so.

The late afternoon sun played on the leaves of the beech tree and a summer breeze sent dappled shadows flickering across the garden far below. Miss Gilpin, lost in her thoughts, drifted with the sunlight and the breeze. She was going to miss this old tree almost as much as she was going to miss her pupils. She would miss the changing colours of the passing seasons and the sound of birdsong that drifted upwards into the rooms at the very top of the house. She was going to miss all of that.

Ten minutes passed and there were no footsteps on the stairs, no knock at the salon door, no Edward! At last, Miss Gilpin turned away from the window, rose from her seat and set off in search of her missing pupil. Edward was never late. Sometimes he was delayed on the stairs if he ran into Mr Lockie, who liked to question him about his progress, but, on the whole, he was always punctual.

Miss Gilpin listened at the top of the staircase. No voices drifted up through the stairwell. Slowly, she made her way down to the next floor, where classes were clearly underway. Marching music seemed to be the order of the day! On the floor below, she paused again but realised that Mr Lockie, in his study, was talking to one of the older pupils about an exam that was coming up. Better not disturb that! Finally, she tip-toed down to the ground floor and looked around her. Of Edward, there was no sign. He always changed into his slippers in the hallway, leaving his outdoor shoes by the hallstand; there were no shoes to be seen. All she could do now was check with Mrs Lockie, who would, no doubt, be down in the kitchen.

"He arrived about fifteen minutes ago, Miss Gilpin. I saw him heading up the stairs as usual," said an anxious Mrs Lockie. "He had his music case with him, just as always. He'd forgotten his slippers today so I didn't even have to wait while he changed out of his shoes. He went straight up the stairs. I can't make any sense of this. Where can he be? Could he be talking with my husband? I know he sometimes stops to have a word."

Miss Gilpin was able to assure her that Edward was not with Mr Lockie and that, as far as she could see, he was not anywhere at all, at least not anywhere in 145, Mapledene Avenue.

A thorough search of the house, with Mr Lockie now involved, quickly established that Edward was nowhere to be found. It was Miss Gilpin who finally said out loud what everyone was thinking. "Edward has run away!" she announced. "There can be no other explanation."

Mr Lockie was quick to agree. "It isn't your fault, Miss Gilpin. Try not to worry. You go upstairs and get ready for your next pupil – Rosemary, I believe – and Mrs Lockie and I will break the dreadful news to Mr Cuthbertson when he comes to collect his son."

Mrs Lockie looked horrified at this prospect. She was always relieved that Edward's father waited at the gate. "I'll leave that to you, dear," she told her husband, stepping further back from the front door, "but I'll be on hand if you need me."

It was at this point that Rosemary came skipping up the path. She was early today and enthusiastic, more than ready for her lesson, the highlight of her week! Miss Gilpin accompanied her upstairs, happy for an excuse to retreat to the safety of her own room and more than content to leave it to her employer to explain to a father that his son had disappeared while in the care of the highly respected Lockie School of Music.

In the end, it was Mr Lockie who did most of the talking. He was a little shorter than Fergal Cuthbertson, who was well over six feet tall, but he had the distinct advantage of being on home ground. Edward's father was always on time and this Friday was no exception. He realised at once that something was wrong when he was invited inside by Mr Lockie. Standing some way behind Mr Lockie, his wife was clearly on the verge of tears as her husband began to explain that Edward was missing. Before he could finish his account of their extensive search of the house, Mr Lockie was interrupted.

"Don't bother wasting any more time on this!" snapped Edward's father. "He's run for it. I reckon he's just done a runner!" He turned to leave. "Don't worry. I'll find him – and when I do, he'll be sorry!" So saying, he stuffed his unread newspaper and the newly purchased copy of *The Eagle* into the Chinese umbrella stand just inside the door and made his exit, leaving a shaken Mr and Mrs Lockie to make the best of it.

With his clenched fists thrust deep into his jacket pockets, he headed off down the path and stood glaring up and down the avenue with a face like thunder.

Mr Lockie followed him. "Don't you think we should inform the police? After all, Mr Cuthbertson, a child is missing."

"No need!" he replied sharply. "I'll deal with this."

Without another word, he turned left along the avenue and crossed over to the opposite pavement. On his way to collect Edward, he'd noticed an elderly man working in his garden. He looked as if he'd been there for a while.

"You been out here all afternoon?" he asked, abruptly.

"Indeed I have," came the reply. "I've been catching up on a few jobs. Got to make progress while the weather's in my favour. Bit breezy but nice and dry today. Why do you want to know?"

"Happen to see a boy with a black leather music case in his hand? Could've been heading this way, probably running, if my guess is right!"

There was a pause. The old man seemed to be struggling to remember. In fact, he was trying to make up his mind about whether or not to give any information at all to this rather large and very angry stranger. He scratched his head and looked up and down the avenue before answering. "I believe I did see a lad with a case. He came out of the music school across the road. You're right. He was running. In fact, he was running as if the devil was on his back! You his dad?"

Fergal Cuthbertson swore under his breath. "Yes, I'm his father, worse luck, and, when I catch up with him, he'll know all about it! He's tried my patience once too often. Which way did he go?"

The old man paused once again. Once more, he looked up and down the length of the avenue before replying. "That way!" he declared with conviction, pointing to his left towards the main road and the shops. "Yes indeed, he went that way!"

Edward's father looked doubtfully in the direction of the old man's pointing finger. "Are you sure? That's the way I went. He'd know I was going that way. He'd hardly run off in the same direction as I was heading! He wouldn't be wanting to run into me. He's on the dodge! He's done a runner!"

The old man stuck to his story. "I know what I saw," he insisted. "He took off along that pavement as if his life depended on it. Maybe he was trying to catch up with you. Maybe he wanted to tell you something. Perhaps he wasn't feeling well."

Edward's father snorted and, without a word of thanks, turned on his heel and set off in the direction from which he'd just come. It didn't make any sense, no sense at all, and yet the old boy had been so sure. Looked as if he had all his marbles, so it had to be true, but why would Edward have risked catching up with him when it was obvious that he was up to something? His father would be the last person he'd want to see. Fergal Cuthbertson's temper bubbled and boiled as, cursing under his breath, he marched off in the direction of the main road, retracing his own steps all the way back to the bus stop. Perhaps, by now, Edward was already at home! Perhaps he'd caught an early bus. If so, he would soon be made to regret it.

At his garden gate, old Bob Harkins watched as Fergal Cuthbertson disappeared into the distance. Job done! He hadn't enjoyed himself so much in years. With a father like that, no wonder the boy had run for his life; he'd have done the same. He'd looked a nice lad and he could certainly move! Mapledene was pretty straight and so he'd had a clear view. The lad hadn't noticed him, hadn't seen him take an interest, but Bob had watched him stop by the school. He'd seen him lift the bike. He'd wondered about that. Still, the lad looked as if he knew where he was going. Pedalled off like mad!

Bob smiled to himself, laughed out loud. Wherever that lad was off to, it certainly wasn't in the same direction that he'd told his bully of a father. He hoped he'd helped him, given the lad a bit more time to put distance between him and whatever trouble he was in. "Well done, Bob, old fellah!" he said out loud to himself. "Now, let's get these tools put away! It's almost time for tea, you old liar."

Jean Cuthbertson was preparing supper when the back door flew open and her husband stormed into the kitchen. Fish cakes and beans, a favourite of Edward's. She always felt he needed something good on a Friday after the dreaded music lesson. It had been a mistake to send him in the first place. She knew that now, but Fergal was adamant that he stuck at it, even after Miss Gilpin had explained to them that Edward was not really cut out to be a pianist. She'd tried, like Miss Gilpin, to make her husband see sense. In the end, she'd given up. It was hopeless.

"Where's Edward? Is he with you?" Fergal's eyes searched the kitchen.

Jean Cuthbertson put down the teapot she was holding in her hand. "What do you mean? He's with you, isn't he?"

"Not now he isn't. He's hopped it! Skipped off when my back was turned. I thought there was a chance he might have helped himself to an early bus home!"

Edward's mum tried to take it in. "Are you saying you don't know where he is? Are you telling me that Edward is missing?"

"Exactly, but when I do know where he is, he'll know all about it!" Without another word, he charged up the stairs; the house shook with the sound of banging doors as Fergal Cuthbertson checked each room in turn. When he came back down to the kitchen, his temper was worse than ever. His wife was close to tears.

"If Edward is missing then we must send for the police. There's a call box at the end of the road. We need to ring for help straight away. Fergal, please do something! Our son is missing. Anything could have happened to him. Goodness knows where he is!"

"I won't be sending for any police so you can forget about that. One way or another, I'll find him – and my first stop will be James McLintock! He'll be involved in this escapade, if I'm not very much mistaken. He's a bad influence!"

Edward's mother dried her eyes with the tea towel. "James is a good lad from a nice family. This won't be his doing. This is down to you, Fergal. Edward is never going to please you and he knows that. Edward's clever. He's done really well at school, but you never give him a good word. He brought some art work home at the end of term. It was outstanding and I don't believe you even looked at it. All that matters to you is that piano. He knows as well as I do that he's never going to be able to play it and that's that! If he's run off, you've driven him to it."

Her words fell on deaf ears. Her husband was in no mood to listen. "We've sacrificed, gone without, so that he could go to the best music school for miles around, and he doesn't appreciate it. Edward's got a brain, but he's bone idle. If he made more of an effort, he could do a sight better than he is doing, but don't you worry I'll see to it that he regrets whatever this is that he's got up to. Make no mistake about that!"

From the living room window, Edward's mother watched as her husband set off in the direction of the McLintocks' shop. As soon as he was out of sight, she grabbed her coat and her purse and ran to the call box on the corner. She often helped out in the shop when things were extra busy, such as at Christmas time when they were short-handed, so their telephone number was one that she knew by heart.

"Sadie!" she shouted as soon as Mrs McLintock answered. "It's Jean. Is Edward with you?"

"No, he isn't. What's happened? What's wrong?"

Faced with the few facts that were available, Mrs McLintock could only turn to James, who clearly knew nothing at all about Edward's disappearance. However, in view of the impending visit from his angry father, James's mum made a point of warning her husband, who was tidying up in the shop, that Fergal was on his way.

James's dad was just about ready to go and collect their fish and chips. "Don't worry! Just make sure that you're both upstairs and out of the way. You two get the table set for supper and I'll deal with Fergal but dealing with him doesn't solve the problem of what's happened to Edward. That's what really worries me. A boy is missing. That's not good news. He needs to be found!"

James and his mum were more than happy to follow Mr McLintock's excellent advice. However, they did leave the main door to the upstairs flat open so that they could listen to what was happening downstairs in the shop. Fergal did have a quick temper that could cause problems for his family, especially if he'd been drinking. Now, however, Mrs McLintock was more concerned for her husband. She needn't have been. Rab McLintock was an imposing figure. He was well over six feet tall, broad at the shoulders and as strong as an ox; as a younger man, he'd tossed the caber at the Highland Show. He was, however, known to be a soft-hearted, gentle giant of a man. His friends, and there were many, knew that he was someone they could count on if they were in trouble. It took him no time at all to send Fergal on his way, telling him in no uncertain terms that he was on the wrong track. Edward was not with James and, in view of that, the sensible thing to do was to inform the police straight away.

"You need to calm down, Fergal. You need to get a grip of yourself and do the right thing by your boy! Get on to the police at once. You can use our phone if you like. It's here in the back shop. You're welcome to use it. Come through. There's no charge. We just need to get the job done. I'll even do it for you if you like."

The response was immediate. "You keep out of this, Rab. I'll deal with it. I'll find Edward all right, without help from you or anyone else. He's my son and my responsibility." So saying, Edward's father left without another word, slamming the door of the shop behind him as he went. The bell rang wildly but, by some miracle, the glass door remained intact.

It was later, when they all sat down to have their Friday supper, that Mrs McLintock said what they'd all been thinking. "Poor Edward," she said. "He probably couldn't face any more of his father and these piano lessons. He's run away. No wonder! Such a shame! Probably got tired of trying to please Fergal. Poor Jean! She'll be worried sick. They used to be so happy but not these days."

James put down his knife and fork. Suddenly, he didn't feel like eating. His mum had once told him that breaking a promise was much worse than breaking the best jug in the house but, now that Edward was missing, he felt he had no choice. It was time. They needed to be told. "Mum! Dad!" he said. "I've got something to tell you. It's important. It's… it's about Edward and his dad."

Chapter 5

A Voyage

Edward woke early. He was amazed that he'd been able to sleep at all, but the night had been warm and his windcheater had done its work. The bench seat had been hard but, after a while, he hadn't really noticed that. Now, as dawn broke, he idly watched the oystercatchers picking their way across the narrow strip of sand. He could hear the lapping of the tide against the sea wall. The water was calm, calmer than he'd known it before. He was relieved about that.

He checked his watch. That was good. It was too soon to make his way back along the promenade. All he had to do, at least for now, was keep out of sight and wait. The morning was growing lighter by the second and all around him was the sound and smell of the sea and the clattering of the gulls. He liked that best of all. He was content to pass his time exactly where he was. A milk float trundled along the esplanade immediately behind him, making brief stops at the hotels as it travelled the length of the seafront, and a bright red post-office van cruised along in the direction of the ferry terminal. Mail for the islands, perhaps?

Gazing out over the waves, Edward suddenly caught sight of something far out at sea: a dark silhouette, low in the water, moving slowly in the early morning light, black as ebony, smooth as silk, heading out towards the open sea and deeper waters. At first, he wasn't sure but, as he watched its steady progress towards the horizon, he could clearly make out the unmistakeable, sleek lines of a submarine. The conning tower rose up like a shark's fin as it cut through the waves. The Americans had come to the sheltered depths of the sea loch further north; this had to be one of the new nuclear subs that patrolled these waters and the ocean beyond. Wow! If only James could be here! It was a moment in time, a moment that he would always remember. As he kept watch, the dark shape slipped slowly out of sight. He couldn't be sure whether it had dived beneath the waves or simply disappeared over the horizon's rim. It reminded him that soon he would also be beyond that same horizon. It was time to think about making a move.

There was no need to rush so Edward took his time, gathered his few possessions together and strolled slowly along the front towards the terminal at the southern end of the prom. The ferry was already waiting by the jetty and a few enthusiastic birdwatchers, weighed down with cameras and binoculars, were preparing to board. The ferryman let them on even though he was in no hurry to cast off; he was ready for his breakfast in the cafe and there would be no departure until he'd finished his bacon and eggs. There would be no bacon and eggs for Edward; he was not a good sailor. He did order some toast and a hot drink. That would do for now. A hasty visit to the washroom enabled him to clean his teeth, wash his face and generally tidy up. He'd packed all he needed to make himself presentable; he wanted to look his best. He combed his hair, made sure that his case was firmly fastened and went off to buy his ticket.

Once on board the ferry, he found a seat behind the bird watchers and took out his copy of *The Eagle*. By now, he more or less knew it by heart; he'd read it so many times. Soon, the ferryman was ready to cast off. Several other passengers had clambered on board and a large sack of mail had been dumped close to the stern, where a metal crate, containing a very large and extremely cantankerous ram, had been loaded earlier. Interesting cargo! The curled horns were impressive.

A boy travelling alone might have attracted attention and Edward had been concerned about that but, thankfully, the birdwatchers were so busy exchanging tales about previous expeditions that they failed to notice him at all. The other passengers seemed more interested in catching up on their sleep and had an air of boredom that suggested this voyage was a frequent experience, one that now held little excitement for any of them. Edward wondered where they were going and why. The ferry would be calling at several islands. He knew that one of them was home to a whisky distillery and decided that these were probably some of their workers. They certainly didn't look like tourists.

Glad that he'd decided against the bacon and eggs, Edward tried to avoid looking out over the rolling waves as the ferry reached open water and began to lurch with the swell. The cabin was warm and comfortable, but the windows soon misted up as the vessel forged ahead through the waves, the rising spray battering against the window panes as the ferryman negotiated the choppy waters. He seemed unconcerned so Edward wasn't afraid. Presumably, it was always like this. In any case, the radio was on and was tuned to a breakfast programme so he tried to distract himself by listening to that, but it wasn't easy because of the chattering of the birdwatchers. He hoped that they were much quieter when they were watching the birds!

It was, as Edward had expected, about ninety minutes before the island came into view. At first, it was small and far away but, happily, its familiar shape grew larger and clearer by the minute. He hoped it hadn't changed, that it would be exactly as he remembered. He packed away *The Eagle* and made sure that he had a firm hold of his case. By the time they'd reached the harbour, he'd made his way to the exit door ahead of everyone else on board and was poised, ready for the signal to disembark. The ferryman seemed to notice him as if for the first time.

"You're in a hurry, young man." He beamed at Edward, a broad grin that spread across his weather-beaten face.

Edward just smiled and nodded. "We'd better let you off first then, hadn't we? Get ready to jump!" There was a judder as the ferry came to a halt, its engines, like the radio, suddenly silent and still.

As soon as the door slid back, Edward jumped. "Thank you!" he called as he ran along the jetty. Glad to be on dry land once again, he hurried towards the red telephone box that stood, just as he'd remembered, close to the harbour wall. He'd written down the number that he needed on a piece of paper just in case he forgot it, even though he knew it off by heart. He looked at his watch. Eight o'clock. They must be awake by now. He only had a few coins for the box so he hoped he would get through straight away. Unfortunately, It wasn't James who answered.

"Edward?" It was Mrs McLintock. "Where are you? Are you all right?" He'd hoped it would be James.

"I'm fine, thank you, Mrs McLintock but, please, I need to speak to James. It's important that I speak to James!" Edward had to put more money into the box while James was summoned. This was not going quite as smoothly as he'd hoped.

"Edward? Where are you? What's going on?" James sounded worried.

Edward tried to keep calm. "James, I can't tell you where I am, not yet, but I want you to let my mum know that I'm safe. She needs to know where to find me so you have to listen really hard. I only have a few coins so please listen carefully and tell Mum what you can hear – not Dad, just Mum. It's very important, James. Don't say anything!

Just listen as hard as you can and tell my mum what you can hear!"

Opening the door of the telephone box, Edward held the receiver skywards for half a minute and then his money ran out. He had no more change. He'd done his best. Now, all he could do was trust that James would play his part.

From the sea's edge, it was a short walk to Harbour Cottage. He'd seen it from the ferry, watched it growing larger as they approached the shore. He was almost there! When the front door opened and he saw his grandfather's familiar face, gazing down at him in absolute amazement, he knew that he was safe.

In Craigbank, however, James was staring at the telephone receiver that was still in his hand as he attempted to make sense of what Edward had told him to do. It sounded important but, despite the obvious fact that Edward was safe, which was the news that everyone had been waiting for, there was now something that had been entrusted to him and he had no idea what to make of it. His mum stood waiting for him to offer some explanation but none was forthcoming.

"Why couldn't he just tell me where he was?" asked James. "He could have said where he was, but he just told me to listen."

Suddenly, they heard the sound of someone at the front door of the shop. Rab McLintock was on hand to open it for Edward's mum, who was in the porch tapping urgently on the glass.

"Thank goodness, you're here!" called James's mum, hurrying through from the back shop. "We've just had a call from Edward. Just five minutes ago! We weren't long downstairs. He's safe, Jean. You needn't worry any more. He's safe."

Jean Cuthbertson closed her eyes. She swayed from side to side and looked, for a moment, as if she were going to faint. She reached out a hand to steady herself and held on to the edge of the counter.

Rab McLintock hurried to fetch a chair. "Sit yourself down, Jean. Sadie'll make you a cup of tea. You just sit there and get your breath back."

Finally, Edward's mum found her voice. "Oh, thank goodness! I actually came to apologise for any trouble that Fergal caused last night," she explained. "I can imagine what it must have been like. He was in such a temper! I told him that James would've had nothing to do with Edward running off, but he wouldn't listen to me. He never does! I never expected to hear that Edward had been on the phone to you. I can hardly take it all in. Thank goodness he's safe, but where is he? Where's he got to?"

A few early-morning customers had begun to arrive and so Mr McLintock was left to mind the shop while the others made their way upstairs, where Edward's mum was settled in an armchair with a hot drink beside her. She looked relieved but shaken all at the same time. Mrs McLintock looked meaningfully at James and he knew he would have to try to make some sense of what Edward had asked him to do. It was up to him now!

"Mrs Cuthbertson," he began, "Edward wouldn't tell me where he was. I don't know why. I don't think he wanted to give too much away to me, but he obviously wanted you to know that he was safe and he asked me to speak to you, not to his dad, just to you. He told me to listen and tell you exactly what I could hear. He said you'd know then where he was. He didn't say anything else so I just listened and then the phone went dead. I think he must have run out of money for the box."

Edward's mum looked just as anxious and confused as James felt. This was not going well. The two mums looked at each other and then back at James.

"Well, James," prompted his mum. "What could you hear?"

James looked uneasy. "I could hear people talking and somebody was laughing, but they seemed far away; I couldn't make out what they were saying. I heard a sheep. Well, I think it was a sheep. I might have heard a horn of some kind, but I'm not sure. It was nearly impossible to make anything out. I'm sorry. I tried really hard, but it was so noisy! Seagulls, I think."

"Seagulls?" Mrs Cuthbertson put down her cup of tea. "Did you say 'seagulls'?" James nodded.

Mrs Cuthbertson sighed a sigh of relief as tears began to run down her face. "Sorry, James. I'm so sorry. It was the gulls you were meant to hear. The other things didn't matter. It was the gulls, you see. They were Edward's message to me. I know exactly where he is now. It's where we should all have gone long, long ago."

No one had noticed Rab McLintock at the door of the sitting room. His customers had gone on their way and he'd made his way quietly upstairs to find out what was happening. "Seagulls, indeed!" He raised his eyebrows.

"Now we all know, don't we? How is Angus? Is he still running the post office up there?"

Edward's mum nodded. "Last I heard, he was, but Fergal doesn't like me writing too often. I wanted to get the phone put in so I could call home, but he says we can't afford it. You know what he's like!"

Although everyone else seemed to understand what had happened, James still had no idea where Edward had got to. He wasn't sure that he understood the full picture, but there was something he knew that he had to say. He'd told his mum and dad and now it was time to tell Edward's mum. He took a deep breath. "Mrs Cuthbertson, Edward doesn't want his dad to know where he's gone. He only wants you to know where he is. I think he's afraid of his dad because he hits him. I saw it happening one day when I came to your house. Mr Cuthbertson was very angry about something. I don't know what it was, but he was hitting Edward and Edward was crying. Edward made me promise not to tell anyone about it but now I just think I've got to."

There was an awkward silence before Jean Cuthbertson answered. "I'm sorry you had to see that, James. I'm afraid that not all dads are as patient as yours. Just lately, things have not been going very well. All three of us have suffered but no one more than Fergal himself. He is not a bad man, but he is a very unhappy man. However, it was wrong of him to take it out on Edward. I should have done something about all of this a long time ago. I should have been stronger. I'm partly to blame so try not to think too badly of Edward's dad. Still, it's never too late to make amends. I know exactly what I need to do now." She leaned back in her chair and James thought how tired she looked.

Mrs McLintock poured a second cup of tea and told Jean to stay as long as she wanted. "Take your time," she said. "You've had quite a morning of it, but the good news is that Edward has come to no harm. That's the main thing. He's safe with Angus. You know that."

James had to know. Everyone else appeared to know. Finally, he asked the question. "So, where is Edward and is Angus his grandfather? I think he told me about him once."

It was Rab who answered. "Yes, he is. Edward 's headed for his grandfather on Seal Island. Angus runs the post office up there, has done for years, and, in his spare time, he's a warden at the gull colony. He took that up a long time ago after Edward's gran died. It was something to do. Angus is a fine chap. Edward will be safe with him. The island is famous for its gulls so the noise was Edward's clue for his mum. He would know that, when you told Jean about the noise of the seagulls, she would know exactly where he'd gone."

"Edward must have been very unhappy to run off to his grandfather like this," said Jean Cuthbertson. "He's had enough and so have I! I need to go. I need to be with Edward. If he can disappear then so can I. Too much time has been wasted already! We should never have left the island." She paused for a moment before continuing. "I know that Fergal was a different man when we lived on the island. He was happy there and so was I, but that was a very long time ago."

Mr and Mrs McLintock exchanged glances. They seemed to come to an unspoken agreement.

"If you really are going ahead with this, Jean," said Sadie McLintock, "then you're going to need help. We all know what Fergal's temper can be like. As you say, he's not a bad man, but he's in a bad way at the moment and he's certainly not going to stand idly by while you leave without him. You can't possibly manage all of this on your own. When are you planning to go?"

"Tomorrow!" The response was immediate. "But Fergal mustn't have a clue about what I'm planning. Once I've found Edward and sorted things out, I'll make sure that Fergal has a chance to put things right but, in the meantime, I daren't tell him anything. Not yet! He wants Edward to be a musician just as he is. It seems to have taken over his life so much so that he's not thinking straight. Edward hates the piano, thanks to Fergal, and, to be honest, I've come to hate the thing as well – and I used to love music. Still, I'd better go. I need to make a start or I'll never be ready in time to catch the early morning ferry."

Jean Cuthbertson got to her feet and gave James a hug before turning towards the door at the top of the stairs. "Thank you, James. You've been a great help to Edward and to me. You've helped me to make up my mind about what needs to be done. Tomorrow, I will do what I should have done a long time ago. I'm going home!"

"Hang on!" interrupted James's dad. "Tomorrow it is, Jean, if that's what you think is best, but this is too much for you on your own. You're going to need some help, so we'd all better put our heads together and work out how it's going to be done. What we need now is a plan – and it's going to have to be a good one."

Chapter 6
The Wild Goose Chase

Rab McLintock was the first to notice that Edward's father was standing in the bus shelter directly across the road from the shop. He wasn't absolutely sure at first, as the shelter was dark and there was quite a bit of traffic moving in between. It was the usual busy Saturday morning and Rab had customers waiting to be served. Finally, he was sure and excused himself for a few minutes to make a trip upstairs, where James's mum and Jean Cuthbertson were still deep in conversation.

"I don't want to alarm you, Jean, but I'm as sure as I can be that Fergal is hanging around in the bus shelter across the road. He may still be thinking that James has got something to do with Edward's disappearance. Anyway, he's watching the shop so, if you want to avoid him, it would be a good idea to leave by the back way. You'll have to squeeze past the van, which is parked in the lane."

Rab hurried back downstairs to attend to his customers. One last quick glance in the direction of the bus shelter told him that he'd been right. Despite the fact that there was a regular bus service and several buses had been and gone by now, the unmistakeable figure of Fergal Cuthbertson still loitered in the shadows.

"I suppose he might have followed me, Sadie," whispered Mrs Cuthbertson, her voice lowered as if her husband could hear her every word, "but he was fast asleep and snoring when I left. He'd been up drinking until late last night, so I was pretty sure he wouldn't be getting up early. No! I'm sure he didn't see me go. He'll think I'm at the laundry because I always pick up my wages on a Saturday morning. In fact, that's where I will be going next but, if you don't mind, I will take Rab's advice and leave by the back way. Fergal is at boiling point and I don't want any more trouble. He shouldn't be here at all. I've told him that James would never be involved in something like this, but he won't listen to me."

"Right you are," replied Sadie McLintock. "Best to do as Rab suggests and leave by the back lane. Better if Fergal doesn't know we've been talking."

Suddenly, James spoke up, which was a surprise for the two mums. They'd forgotten that he was still in the room. "Excuse me, Mrs Cuthbertson, but I think I might have an idea. If Mum could help me with a few things, I might be able to keep Mr Cuthbertson busy for an hour or two – if that would help you to do whatever you have to do. I'd like to do something to help Edward."

Wide eyed, the two women listened to James's plan. When he'd finished talking, they looked at each other and simultaneously said the same thing, "Brilliant!"

A few simple preparations were necessary before James could make his departure by way of the front door of the shop. After very obviously looking to the right and to the left along the high street, he set off purposefully in the direction of the playing fields at the far end of town – The Reccy! He appeared to pay absolutely no attention whatsoever to the bus shelter across the road but, out of the corner of his eye, he saw Edward's father leave his post and, keeping to the opposite side of the road, set off in the same direction as himself. So far, so good! He was following, just as James had intended him to do. However, James knew that this was not a game. Edward's mum was depending on him. He had to get this right. He had to keep a cool head and keep to his plan.

Fergal, meanwhile, congratulated himself. He'd been right all along. Through the grimy windows of the shelter, he'd watched James McLintock look both ways before heading off at a lively pace. He'd noticed that, in his hand, James was carrying a small, green, leather suitcase, the kind that people use when they're staying overnight somewhere. There was no way that James would be going off on his own to stay anywhere. That meant that there had to be some other reason for the case. Fergal was as sure as he could be that he knew what that reason was. Edward was hiding somewhere and James was helping him to stay out of sight. All he had to do was follow the suitcase and it would lead him straight to Edward, wherever he might be. It was simple. All he had to do was keep out of sight.

As the playing fields drew nearer, James slackened his pace and Fergal did likewise, keeping several yards and several pedestrians between himself and his quarry. He was taking no chances of being seen. Finally, James turned in through the gates of the deserted recreation ground and took the main path that led past the running track, keeping to the direct route that led straight to the pavilion. Fergal gritted his teeth. The pavilion! Why hadn't he thought of that? The boys spent hours here every week. It was an obvious place for Edward to hide. He cursed himself under his breath for not thinking of it before.

From behind the shed, where the greenkeepers kept their tools, Fergal watched as James made his way up the broad flight of steps at the front of the building. At the top, the boy paused to remove a large key from his jacket pocket. Once the door was opened, James and the suitcase disappeared inside.

Built in the nineteen-thirties, the pavilion was an imposing structure, almost too grand for this part of town and certainly very much too grand for a small recreation ground. It wouldn't have looked out of place on a racecourse or on the seafront of a fashionable holiday resort. Painted creamy white, it had three floors with a wide balcony on the third floor. It was topped by a flat roof that had the unfortunate habit of letting in the rain. Fergal had never been inside the building before, but there was a first time for everything!

Once James was safely inside, it was time to make his move. Breaking into a run, Fergal Cuthbertson headed straight for the main entrance. To his relief, the door was still unlocked. Once inside, he paused briefly in the hallway so that he could listen for voices or any sound that would tell him which way to go. He was met by stony silence.

Even though it was summer, the interior was bleak, filled with the cold, creeping damp that is often found where concrete walls and empty rooms conspire to create a pervading, unwelcoming chill. To his right, the kitchen door lay half open. Peering into the room, he could see that it was empty, except for a tray of oranges on the table and a clean tea towel spread out neatly over the cooker top.

The room on his left was also completely empty. It was obviously used for meals as four long wooden tables were in position, as were several piles of folding chairs, but there was no real sign of any activity; the tables were bare. Quietly, Fergal made his way up to the first floor, where the changing rooms and the showers were also empty. Now he knew! All that was left were the upstairs rooms. These were meeting rooms, seldom used except on very special occasions, at least that was what he'd heard. This was new territory for him. The Reccy was not a place that Fergal was in the habit of visiting very often. Another reason why it would appeal to Edward!

Each of the three doors on the top landing was thrown back with force but, to his surprise and disappointment, Fergal found that each room was just as empty as the one before. At the front, he tried the glass doors that led out on to the balcony but they were securely locked. In any case, he could clearly see that the balcony was just as empty as the rest of the pavilion appeared to be. There was no sign of Edward and, much to his surprise, there was no sign of James. Every room was cold and empty.

To be absolutely certain, he checked each room again before making his way downstairs once more. Of Edward, there was indeed no sign, nor was there any trace of anyone else. It made no sense. As he drew level with the kitchen on the ground floor, he noticed that the door had been opened more widely and, on the kitchen table, next to the tray of oranges, lay the small, green, leather suitcase that James had been carrying. Apart from that, the room was just as it had been before.

On entering the kitchen, he noticed what looked like a cupboard door tucked away in the corner to his left. Peering inside, he expected to find one or both of the boys but found neither. It was just a pantry, well stocked with cups and saucers, plates and bowls and several tins of biscuits, some unopened, but nothing else. Stepping right inside, he saw a notice. It was pinned to the door frame by two rusty drawing pins. When he looked more closely, he could see that it was just a list of dates for forthcoming football matches and meetings of the running club. It was of no interest at all. Fergal returned to the kitchen, kicking the pantry door shut behind him. Looking out of the window, he could see that the playing fields were deserted. There was no sign of anyone and so he turned his attention to the small, green suitcase that sat in the middle of the kitchen table.

It took only a few moments to undo the brown, leather strap that was tightly wrapped around the case. He undid the metal buckle that held it in place and opened the lid. It fell back quite easily to reveal its contents: six red and white football strips, clean and neatly folded, as well as half a dozen pairs of freshly laundered striped socks! On top of this collection was a note in Sadie McLintock's handwriting: 'Hope the match goes well this afternoon. Mrs Colquhoun has very kindly agreed to wash the strips next week. She'll collect them after the game.'

Fergal Cuthbertson slammed the suitcase shut and threw the leather strap across the kitchen. It sent the tea towel flying from the hob and created an unwelcome draught in an already cold room. Time to call it a day! A wild goose chase, after all! Returning to the main exit, he realised that the main door was now firmly shut. Rattling it failed to make any impact. It was rock solid. Locked! There was no sign of a key on a hook anywhere and, what's more, there was no sign of James McLintock. The boy had been delivering football strips. Nothing more. Presumably, he was now well on his way home. Perhaps Jean was right after all. Perhaps James really didn't have anything to do with Edward's disappearance. His whole morning had been a pointless waste of valuable time and now he was stuck in this dismal kitchen until someone arrived to open the pavilion in time for the afternoon match.

James was elsewhere. He was well on his way! While Fergal Cuthbertson was considering how he might explain his presence to whoever came to unlock the door, James was already safely seated beside his father in the delivery van that was parked, just out of sight, behind the tangled hawthorn hedge that surrounded the playing fields. Edward's father had been so intent on keeping James in sight that he'd failed to notice that someone else was keeping a watchful eye on him!

James had quite enjoyed the first part of his plan. The suitcase at the top of the stairs had given him his idea. It had been his mum's turn to wash the strips and he often delivered them for her. She had her own key. However, inside the pavilion and holding his breath in the cold darkness of the pantry, the suitcase ready in his hand, he'd been afraid. He'd listened to Edward's father climbing the stairs to the floors above. He'd heard the sound of his feet on the bare stone steps. From his hiding place, he'd heard the slamming of the upstairs doors and used the opportunity, as planned, to put the case in an obvious position on the kitchen table. Fergal had been making so much noise by that time that he hadn't heard the rattle of the key in the lock as James closed the heavy entrance door behind him. Then, he'd taken to his heels and run as fast as he could to the van that would be waiting for him just behind the hedge. He had to hope that he'd created enough time for Edward's mum to make a start on her preparations. The footballers wouldn't open up until much later on in the afternoon, which would provide her with a few hours, but no more. After that, Fergal would be on the loose and, in all probability, in an even worse temper than before.

Fortunately, everything had gone smoothly. Safely on his way home in the van, he was now as high as a kite and in a hurry to recount his adventure in great detail to his mum, who was holding the fort back at the shop.

As his dad waited for the traffic lights to change to green, James took the opportunity to ask a question that had been in his mind ever since that dreadful day in the hallway. "Dad, why is Edward's dad the way he is? He's just a bully and he can't have any friends. He's not very nice to Edward. What's the matter with him?"

"Well," replied Mr McLintock, driving on as the lights changed, "he wasn't always like he is. Maybe he should have stayed on the island. We knew him slightly back then and he seemed a decent chap. When he came here, he got a job in the shipyard, on the cranes, but he got the sack. It was very sad and a bit silly. He stole a steak pie from the canteen. Actually, he and a pal stole one each, just for a prank, I suppose. They got caught but, while the other lad took his telling off and got back to work, Fergal lost his temper and punched somebody. That was that! He was sacked on the spot! He was never the same man after that. Just went from bad to worse!" After a moment's thought, Rab added, "You mustn't let Edward know that I've told you about all of this. I'm not sure that he was ever told the truth about what had happened. Anyway, Fergal used his musical skills to keep food on the table and poor Jean has had to keep going in several jobs that don't pay very much at all."

Later, in his room, James thought about what his dad had said. To his own surprise, he found himself feeling sorry for Mr Cuthbertson. He thought of him now, locked in the pavilion. It would be pretty cold. It was always cold, even in summer. Still, the football teams would be arriving at about two-thirty and Steve, who ran the football club, would be opening up the pavilion beforehand so that everyone could get into their kit. Steve would let him out. He wondered how Fergal would explain how he came to be there in the first place. James hoped he wouldn't be punching anyone else!

In the chill of the pavilion, Edward's dad was also doing some serious thinking. He'd tried all the doors, several times, including the ones that led out on to the balcony on the top floor. Hopeless! Finally, he decided to sit it out. There was nothing else for it. After a while, he switched on the ancient oven in the kitchen and left the door wide open so that the heat would escape into the kitchen. It helped. He brought a chair through from the room next door, put the kettle on to make a cup of tea and helped himself to some of the biscuits in a tin that had already been opened. The notice on the wall in the pantry informed him that a match was scheduled for two-thirty so, presumably, someone would open up before then. He would just say he'd brought the football kits and decided to wait until they were collected. It would sound a bit lame, but it would have to do.

Outside the window, the sun shone over the playing fields. Fergal was not very familiar with this place. He'd turned up a couple of times to watch Edward running. He could go like the wind. On each occasion, Edward had gone home with a trophy, and he'd been proud of his son. He suddenly felt ashamed that he hadn't told him so. Now, of course, Edward was gone. Gone where? That was a question he wished he could answer. Perhaps Jean was right yet again. Perhaps it was time to get help from the police. However, there would be questions and some of those questions would be difficult to answer. Why would a perfectly ordinary schoolboy decide to give his father the slip and run off to who knows where without any warning and without telling anybody where he was going or why? There would be questions for him, for Jean, for The Lockie School of Music and, without a doubt, questions for Edward's best friend. He worried most of all about what James might say. Lately, he'd lost his temper and raised his hand to Edward. Beaten by his own father when he'd been a small boy, he was deeply ashamed of the fact that history had repeated itself. James McLintock had seen him at his worst. All in all, he thought it would be best if he could avoid all those difficult questions and find Edward on his own.

By the time Steve Alexander arrived to prepare for the afternoon match, Fergal Cuthbertson had switched off the oven, cleared away the crumbs and tidied the kitchen. As he left, he waved to the teams as they were arriving to change into their gear. "All the best!" he shouted casually over his shoulder as he headed for the gate. "Hope the game goes well!"

"Who was that?" enquired one of the mums.

Steve looked puzzled. "I have no idea," he replied. "I have no idea whatsoever."

By three o'clock, Jean Cuthbertson was on watch at her sitting room window. By now, she guessed, someone would have let Fergal out of the pavilion. He'd be on his way home. James had given her the gift of time and she had used that time well. Two suitcases, hastily packed, were now tucked away under her bed and, thanks to Sadie and Rab McLintock, her plans were in place for the following day. Everything now depended on what happened in the next hour or so.

Finally, Jean saw her husband's familiar figure come into view. Cruel though it seemed, she would have to convince him that, like him, she was still unaware of Edward's whereabouts. That was the first challenge. After that, she would have to play it by ear. It was highly unlikely that he would say anything about following James and being locked in the pavilion for a couple of hours. He wouldn't want her to know about that.

"It's no good, Jean, there's no sign of him anywhere. Tomorrow, I'll have one more try and, if there's still no sign of him, we'll have to go to the police. There's nothing else for it." Edward's father threw himself down on the nearest armchair and took off his shoes. "My feet are killing me," he said, "but tomorrow I'm heading back to that music school. That silly old duffer in the garden sold me a pup. Talking a load of rubbish. I'm sure of it. Anyway, I'll be heading off in exactly the opposite direction, just to see if I can work it all out. There's something here that I'm not seeing. Edward's played me for a fool but, while I may be many things, I'm certainly not that! Tomorrow, one way or another, I'm going to get to the bottom of all of this."

From the sideboard by the fireplace, Fergal took out a bottle of whisky. After pouring himself a large glass, he sat down in the chair next to the window. While he drank, he kept an eye out for anyone coming along the road as if, at any moment, Edward might suddenly appear. Jean Cuthbertson went through to the kitchen to make a cup of tea. She supposed that she should be making something for them to eat, but she didn't think that either of them would feel like any supper. Despite the warmth of the afternoon, she shivered.

Chapter 7
Bicycles and Buses

Jean Cuthbertson awoke on Sunday morning to find that her husband, unusually for a Sunday, was already up, dressed and in the kitchen. Even more surprising was the fact that he'd set the table for breakfast and was already making a pot of tea. "You're all set, then?" she asked, putting two slices of bread under the grill. Fergal just nodded. He looked a broken man and Jean had to work hard not to change her mind and tell him the truth about Edward. Still, she'd decided what to do and there was no going back now.

Breakfast, such as it was, was eaten in silence. Finally, it was Jean who broke the ice. "What exactly are you planning to do, Fergal?"

There was a pause while her husband slowly rose to

his feet and put on his jacket. "Like I said last night, I'm heading up to town to follow the path that I think Edward probably took. Who knows where he's gone, but I aim to do my level best to find out. Failing that, I'll do what you want and go down to the police station tomorrow morning and see what they can do."

Jean nodded. "When do you think you'll be back?"

Again, there was a pause. "Not sure. This may be a complete waste of time, but there's something I'm missing in all of this and I'm sure that the answer lies in Mapledene Avenue. That's where all this trouble began so that is where I aim to start. This cannot go on. Edward has to be found."

Jean watched as her husband set off down the hill towards the bus stop. Despite all that had happened, she felt sorry for him. His broad shoulders drooped and he looked exhausted. She wondered if he'd slept at all. She almost ran after him to tell him that his journey wasn't necessary, that Edward was safe and sound, that he could stop searching because his runaway child was with his grandfather, with Angus. Somehow, she stopped herself. Too much had gone wrong and, at the moment, Fergal was unpredictable. He didn't seem to be in control of himself and she was afraid of what he might do. She had to reach Edward first. After that, she would do her best to put things right with Fergal. Seal Island might offer a solution for them all. She'd been giving that some thought, but there was no point in making any plans. Not yet!

Once the breakfast things were cleared away, Mrs Cuthbertson walked around her house for what she thought might be the very last time. They'd been happy there for a while but not as happy as they'd been on the island, which had been their first home. After Fergal had lost his job, things had got worse. She'd hoped the piano might have helped but, instead of that, there had been rows and Edward's life had become a misery. She should have stepped in, made Fergal see sense, made him accept that he needed to let Edward be himself. She hadn't done enough to help her son. She needed to help him now. There could be no going back. She pulled the two heavy suitcases out from under the bed and humped them downstairs. It was a bit of a struggle. Finally, putting on her coat, she paused just long enough to pack her wages and a few small bits and pieces into her handbag. It was only a short walk to the telephone box and then back to sit at the foot of the stairs and wait for Rab McLintock and his delivery van. In a few minutes, she would be on her way. In a few hours, she would be with Edward and her own father. Soon, she would be on Seal Island, where she belonged.

Fergal Cuthbertson spent the entire bus journey turning over and over in his mind all that had happened but, no matter how often he did so, he could make no sense of any of it. He'd known that Edward hated the music school but he'd hoped that, if he kept his nose to the grindstone, things might improve. He knew now that he'd been wrong. He'd had to admit that to himself, if not yet to anyone else. Now, the most important person he needed to tell was Edward - but he was missing! It was a sobering thought. The world could be a dangerous place for a boy on his own.

Once outside the music school, Fergal tried to put himself in Edward's shoes. He looked back along Mapledene Avenue in the direction that the old man had indicated. That didn't make any sense. He should have ignored the old fool. No boy with a brain would have followed his father if he was in the mood to run away from him. That would be crazy. It was his own fault. He should never have listened. It was time to start again.

Turning to face the other way, he could see the avenue stretching into the distance as far as the eye could see. On his left were the tall town houses that dominated the view but, to his right, was the private school with its vast playing fields taking up acres of land beyond the buildings themselves. He walked slowly past the gates, which were closed and padlocked. The place would be closed for the summer holidays now, but it had certainly been open on the previous Friday. He recalled that there had been some sort of sporting event in full flow; he'd heard the yells and screams of the boys when he'd gone to collect Edward.

A notice, attached to one of the iron gates, caught his eye and he stopped to read it, but it didn't seem to have any bearing on his search for answers. Apparently, a bicycle had been stolen from the gateway on Friday afternoon. There was a very full description and the offer of a generous reward for anyone who could help to return it to its owner. The notice informed any reader that the bike in question was red with a parcel rack at the rear and a basket attached to the front handlebars. Edward had wanted a new bike. Fergal thought about that and wished now that he'd bought one for him. He had the money saved already. Just another thing he'd got wrong! The list was getting longer.

The avenue was quite grand in its own way, with expensive houses to the left and playing fields to the right. In the distance, he thought he could make out the ringing of church bells. Sunday morning. Sunday prayers. It had been a long time since Fergal Cuthbertson had said his prayers – but he was praying now, praying that he would find his son, praying that he had come to no harm.

At the end of Mapledene Avenue was the junction with the busy road that passed in front of the Art Gallery and Museum. Fergal approached the gallery through the car park. Few people were about despite the fact that it was the weekend. It was a sunny day, so perhaps there were other things that people were more interested in doing. Fergal stared at the enormous building, with its turrets and wide stone steps that led up to a grand entrance flanked by marble columns. Could Edward have hidden himself in there? He liked museums. Could he be inside?

Deciding that there was nothing to be lost by having a walk round, Fergal crossed the car park and headed for the main doorway. As he approached the stone steps, he noticed, neatly parked in one of the metal racks, a bright red bicycle. It had a parcel shelf at the rear and a wicker basket attached to the front handlebars! Edward could run. No doubt about that. Still, a bicycle would've helped. A bicycle would have made his exit so much quicker. Stroke of luck, perhaps? He would have reached this spot in no time. Nevertheless, the bike had been left here for someone to find. Perhaps he'd hoped that it would be the owner – unless, of course, Edward was still around and planning to come back for it. Was he somewhere around? Was he watching him at this very moment?

For what seemed like hours, but was in fact no more than forty minutes, Edward's father, from his vantage point at the top of the steps, watched the comings and goings of a growing number of visitors but to no avail. There was no sign of his son and an hour long search of the museum had been a complete waste of time.

As he left, he saw that the bicycle was still in place. He thought about wheeling it back to the school gates as he retraced his steps but decided against it. What if he was barking up the wrong tree? Best not to get involved. He left it where it was and retraced his steps towards Mapledene Avenue. At the junction, he paused to take a long look around him. There were now streams of traffic going in all directions and crowds of people milling about, some nervously trying to cross the road at the traffic lights, while others were hurrying along the far pavement towards the bus stop. A double-decker was just arriving and several families were queuing up to board it. They looked like holiday-makers. The adults were laughing and calling to each other as they herded their children on to the bus. They were laden down with picnic baskets, windbreaks and buckets and spades – and they looked happy. Fergal turned away. He envied them.

It had all been for nothing. Making his way back along the avenue, past the entrance to the music school and the school gates, Fergal cast his mind back over everything he'd seen. He was as sure as he could be that he'd followed the route taken by Edward two days earlier and yet he'd found no clue as to where his son might be. He was no closer to finding him.

Slowly, he made his way along the pavement, thankful for the trees that provided some shade, sheltering him from the rising heat of the summer afternoon. His throat felt dry. He wondered if Edward was thirsty or hungry. Where was he at this very moment? Did he have any money? Where was he sleeping? Was he safe? Was he hurt? The questions went round and round in unrelenting circles, but no answers were forthcoming. One question that he did not need to ask himself was 'Why?' He knew the answer to that one.

As he reached the bus stop, he had to step back; the first bus was not the one he wanted. He double-checked the destination board and then kept well out of the way so that other people could get on. Three women disembarked. They were dressed in their best and looked as if they were on their way to church, but he paid them little attention. Something else had caught his eye. It was the destination board on the bus that was now drawing away from the stop. He couldn't quite place what it was – but he had the feeling that he'd missed something, something important.

The bus was heading for one of the vast housing estates on the edge of the city, nothing unusual or special in any way. However, as he continued to wait for his own transport to arrive, he knew that the destination board had reminded him of something and, for the life of him, he couldn't figure out what it was. Somewhere along the way, he'd missed something – but what? All the way home, in his mind, he revisited every step he'd taken, but it was hopeless.

Turning his key in the lock, Fergal noticed that his wife's bicycle was still leaning against the shed. She would be waiting, worrying. He would have to tell her that he'd failed, that Edward was still missing, that they would have to contact the police, that she'd been right all along.

He hung up his jacket in the hallway and went straight through to the kitchen at the back of the house. It was still and quiet. A tea tray, set for one, sat in the middle of the kitchen table. When he went back to the living room at the front of the house, he found that it was empty and silent, apart from the loud ticking of the clock. Fergal saw that, apart from that clock, the mantelpiece was bare; the framed photograph of Edward in his school uniform was gone, as were the two silver cups that he'd won for running.

"Jean!" he called out from the foot of the staircase. There was no reply.

As he climbed the stairs, Fergal had a feeling that the floor above would be as empty as the rest of the house – and he was right. The bedrooms, warmed by the heat of the afternoon, seemed just as he would have found them on any ordinary day – but they felt different. Propped up on the dressing table was a note from his wife. He sat down on the edge of the bed to read it.

'I'm sorry, Fergal, but I have to go. Edward needs me. Don't worry any more. He is quite safe. Don't try to find us. I will be in touch with you as soon as I can. Try to understand. There is plenty of food in the pantry. Look after yourself.' Before signing her name at the foot of the letter, Jean had written the single word 'Sorry' once again.

He should have felt anger. He should have – but, above all, the main thing that he felt was relief. Edward was safe and his mother knew where he was. That was what mattered most. A brief search revealed the fact that the two suitcases, which were normally to be found under the bed, were gone, as were many of Jean's clothes; the chest of drawers under the window and the old wardrobe that stood in the corner were half empty. Similarly, it was obvious from a brief look round Edward's room, that Jean had also taken some of his clothes with her. She must have been laden down. Fergal wondered how she'd managed to pack without his noticing and then carry two heavy suitcases all by herself.

Standing at the window of Edward's room, Fergal Cuthbertson looked down the hill towards the bus stop. It was quite a long way for anyone to struggle with two heavy cases, let alone a slightly built woman. Jean must have had help from someone. As he stood there, a picture began to form in his mind. It was of a small, green suitcase! James McLintock and the pavilion! Perhaps that had not been an accident after all. Heavy luggage wouldn't be a problem if you had access to a delivery van and a willing driver! He was as sure as he could be that the McLintocks would know exactly where he could find his wife and his son. Tonight, he needed to think, but first thing tomorrow morning he would be paying a visit to the McLintocks. It was time for answers!

Standing in his son's bedroom, Fergal had to admit to himself that he'd got things wrong and now everybody knew it. It was up to him to put things right if he wanted to get his family back, but it was going to be difficult if he couldn't find Jean and Edward. Rab and Sadie could deny all knowledge of the whole affair. Indeed, Jean might simply have taken a taxi. He could be barking up the wrong tree all over again. Fergal refolded Jean's letter and slipped it into his trouser pocket. His gaze drifted around the walls of the room.

Edward wasn't musical. Fergal had recently come to accept that. He was, however, artistic. His mother had always enjoyed drawing and painting and Edward had taken after her. The walls of the house were lined with pictures, all created by Edward and framed by his proud mother. Some of them were little more than colourful scribbles that Edward had created when he was a toddler; some, however, were more recent. In the last year or two, he'd spent quite a bit of time drawing birds, mostly copying from photographs in a bird book that he'd been given some time ago, or from watching the few birds that visited their tiny garden. The most striking, Fergal thought, was a detailed drawing of a golden eagle's head. It was outstanding. Next to that was a black and white sketch of a barn owl. The eyes seemed to follow you around the room. Finally, his most recent drawing had been of a herring gull, standing like a sentry on guard duty on a grey harbour wall. Fergal seemed to think he'd copied that one from a postcard. The lad was not without ability and he was doing well at school – far better than his father had ever done. Closing the bedroom door behind him, Fergal headed for the stairs. He wondered how much whisky was left in the bottle in the sideboard cupboard.

Half-way down the stairs, he stopped. For a few seconds, he stood rooted to the spot, before turning on his heel and heading back in the direction of Edward's room. Standing in the middle of the floor, he looked around him, pausing to study each of Edward's drawings in turn. Something told him that the answer was not in Mapledene Avenue, after all; it was here in this room. He could feel it in his bones. Somewhere, right in front of him, was the key to Edward's disappearing trick, if only he could work out what it was.

The drawing of the seagull held his gaze. For several minutes, he stared at it. It was as if it wouldn't let him go. Then, all at once, he knew. He knew at last what he'd seen that should have told him exactly where Edward had gone and how he'd done it. He knew at long last what had been staring him in the face. The destination board!

He hadn't bothered to pay too much attention to the details on any of the destination boards on the buses that had passed his stop or, for that matter, the one that had paused to pick up passengers, because he'd known exactly where they'd been going. However, they had reminded him of something else that he'd seen that day. He just hadn't been able to figure out what it was. Now he remembered!

He'd seen the holiday crowds heading for the coast. He'd turned away, but he'd known where they were going because he'd travelled that route many times before. They were heading for the seaside. They were heading for Castle Bay! When Edward had been small, they'd often gone there as a family when the weather was good and the summer days were long. He'd remembered how happy they'd been before he'd lost his job, before money had been short, before he'd started drinking and before the arrival of the piano.

Edward must have borrowed that bike after coming across it at the school gate, used it to help him reach the stop on the main road and catch the tourist bus to Castle Bay. He'd be heading for the coast, but he wouldn't be going to build sandcastles or buy candyfloss or feed the seagulls. Oh no! Fergal knew now exactly what Edward would have had in mind. He would be setting out on a journey that he knew well. Edward would be on his way to catch the West Coast Ferry that would take him out to Seal Island, out to the comforting safety of Harbour Cottage and the welcoming arms of his beloved grandfather. "He's with Angus!" he cried out aloud. "He's with Angus!" Despite himself, he began to laugh. He stood in the empty room and laughed until tears of relief began to trickle down his face.

It didn't take long to pack a few necessities into the haversack that he kept on top of the wardrobe. No need to consult with the McLintocks now. By tomorrow afternoon, he'd be on his way. Fergal made himself a sandwich and went through to the sideboard for the whisky bottle. For a moment, he held it tightly in his hand, took a long look at it and then carried it through to the kitchen, where he removed the cap and poured the contents down the sink.

A clear head was what was needed now. There was much to do.

Before turning in for the night, there was just one more job to do. Fergal reached behind the tallboy in the spare room. For some time, he'd been saving up to pay for that new bike for Edward. He'd decided that the music exam was a lost cause. He was going to buy the bike, anyway. Still, that might have to wait for a bit as he would be needing some of the cash for his fare. The money from his busking and the fees that he earned for playing for weddings and funerals had been tucked safely out of sight in a brown paper bag.

After struggling and failing to get hold of the package, Fergal eased the heavy piece of furniture away from the wall by just a few inches. Something was there. However, it was not what he'd expected to find. The brown paper bag was still there, but its contents had been removed. In place of the money, he found several sheets of music, piano music! Edward's examination pieces! He also found a pair of sheepskin slippers, the slippers that had travelled to and from The Lockie School of Music every Friday afternoon. He'd wondered how his son was managing for money. At least he didn't have to worry about that any more! Edward had outsmarted him at every turn but, surprisingly, he didn't feel angry. No! He couldn't avoid the uncomfortable feeling that he'd got exactly what he deserved.

In his guitar case, he remembered, he would still have the coins from his last busking session. He'd done very well that day so, with luck, it would be enough. The fact that most of it was in small change posed something of an embarrassment – but that wouldn't have to matter. Fergal tipped the coins into an old tobacco pouch and stuffed it into his haversack. It would have to do!

Chapter 8

Seal Island

James had never been on a boat before, not a proper sea-going ferry like *The Skua*. He hadn't been able to believe his good luck when Mrs Cuthbertson had asked his mum and dad if he might be allowed to travel with her and spend a few days with Edward. Now, he watched with growing excitement as Seal Island grew larger and larger with every moment that passed. Above them, the soaring clouds of gulls grew louder and louder, hundreds of them, thousands perhaps, filling the air with their shrill voices. Around him, all he could see were silver wings, dipping and gliding in the morning sun. Mrs Cuthbertson laughed. There was no point in trying to make conversation.

As the ship reached the jetty and the ferryman

sounded the horn, Jean Cuthbertson tugged James's sleeve and pointed in the direction of a long row of stone cottages that overlooked the harbour. Someone was standing on guard at the window of the very first cottage in the row. Even at this distance, they could clearly see that it was Edward. James watched as the door flew open and Edward came tearing down the hill to meet them. He was followed, at a gentler pace, by a large gentleman with wild, grey thistledown hair, a broad smile and a bushy beard that made him look a bit like Father Christmas. He was carrying a sturdy walking stick, which he raised in salute as he made his way down the slope towards them.

While James organised the luggage, Mrs Cuthbertson ran to meet Edward and hugged her son as if she would never let him go. Edward's grandfather reached out and shook James firmly by the hand and took charge of the luggage. He handed his walking stick to James and, with a wink, he signalled to him to follow him up to Harbour Cottage. James had his own things on his back in a canvas rucksack. No words were exchanged as these would have been drowned out by the excited screeching of the gulls and the chattering of the many passengers, who were now disembarking immediately behind them.

Once inside the cottage, with the door firmly closed, it was finally possible for Mrs Cuthbertson to formally introduce James to her father. Grandpa Angus placed the cases down beside the fireplace and shook James's outstretched hand all over again. "I'm very pleased to meet you," he boomed. "Edward has been telling me all about you. He says you're his best friend, a great footballer and that one day you'll play in goal for Scotland! You must call me 'Angus'. Much friendlier than Mr McKenzie."

Edward looked happier than James had seen him in a very long time. As soon as they'd all got settled, Jean helped her father to prepare some lunch for everyone – oatcakes and cheese with home-grown tomatoes – and then suggested that Edward might like to show James around the village so that she and Edward's grandfather could have a talk, sort out the sleeping arrangements and work out what they were all going to have for supper later on. James and Edward were happy to head outdoors towards the harbour once again, where the gulls – and the birdwatchers – were still circling.

James was amazed by the size of Seal Island. It was immediately obvious that it was much bigger than he'd imagined. He found the idea of being on an island exciting, especially as the sun was shining, the air was fresh, everywhere smelled of the sea and there were lots of people everywhere. "It's so busy!" he cried, raising his voice so that he could be heard. "I suppose I thought it would be a quiet place, a rock out in the ocean. I hadn't expected all this."

Edward understood. He remembered his first visit. "It's quieter in the winter, Grandpa says, but the rest of the year there's always something going on. The gull colony brings lots of visitors. Grandpa says it's the largest in the whole of Europe, so people come from hundreds of miles away to see it and take pictures. The television people have been here several times. There are other seabirds as well and then there are the seals that come here to have their pups. Seals have come here for centuries; that's how the island got its name."

As they walked along by the water's edge, James couldn't help noticing how different it was from Castle Bay; there were no amusements or candyfloss sellers or paddle boats. There was nothing like that. Several small fishing boats were anchored in the shelter of the harbour, bobbing at anchor just a short distance out from the shore. Two larger vessels were up on wooden stocks close to the harbour wall and an artist was at work at an easel just outside the post office, focussing on the jetty, where the ferry was already preparing to leave once again. Several people, weighed down with climbing gear, were already boarding for the return journey to the mainland.

As the two boys turned away from the sea and wandered into the village itself, James was surprised to see so many shops, different kinds of shops, just like at home. He'd expected there to be a village store and little else but found quite the opposite. There were all the usual things that tourists expect to see, such as souvenirs, tartan slippers, tweed travelling rugs, postcards, local sweets and shortbread biscuits. However, in addition, there were ordinary shops, the sort that sell useful things that people really need. There was also a library and an art shop.

Edward stopped outside the the art shop and looked longingly at the window display. "I couldn't bring any of my drawing things with me," he said. "I couldn't carry them so I had to leave everything behind, but I'll buy some new things, if Mum says it's OK. I'll have to save up."

Turning to wander back along the beach, which was a mixture of sand and shingle, Edward explained that, when the tide was out, they would be able to search for fossils. "I found two the last time I was here," he announced proudly, "and Grandpa's still got them on his kitchen windowsill. I can't remember what he said they were called, but we can ask him when we get back."

Finally, as they made their way back towards the harbour cottages, James pointed towards the crest of the hill, where he could see the lighthouse that dominated the headland. "Wow!" he cried. " I saw that from the ferry but it looks so much bigger from here!" The colours were fresh and bright and looked as if the building had been recently painted, red and white.

"That's The Seal Light!" exclaimed Edward. "The lighthouse keeper lives in the last cottage in the line. His name's Mr McIver and he's a friend of Grandpa's. He's offered to take me up to the top tomorrow, right up beside the light. Now that you're here, I'm sure he'll say it's OK for both of us to go, if you'd like that."

James was more than happy to agree to that, but he was surprised that Edward was so enthusiastic. "Are you sure you really want to go up?" he asked. "You don't usually like heights."

"I won't be going near the edge of the gallery. You don't need to worry about that," replied Edward. "I think I'm actually more worried about the staircase than being at the top. Mum says it's a spiral that gets narrower and narrower as you get closer to the gallery, so I'm not exactly looking forward to that bit. Still, I'm sure we'll be safe enough with

Mr McIver; he used to be one of the mountain rescue team with Grandpa Angus."

Some climbers were just setting off from the crest of the hill as Edward and James reached Harbour Cottage. "They won't be going far tonight," said Edward. "They'll be heading for the ramblers' hostel ready for tomorrow so they can make an early start on Sutherland Hill. If we look out from the upstairs windows of Grandpa's cottage, we can see it in the distance. It's one of the highest peaks on the island. There aren't any really high mountains here, but there are some hills that are high enough to bring climbers to the island, even in the winter. Grandpa Angus was saying that most people play it safe, but now and again Mountain Rescue have to turn out in the snow when people get stuck. Grandpa used to go up with them so he's got lots of stories to tell. I'll ask him to tell us some after supper tonight."

As they arrived back at Harbour Cottage, Edward's mum was just setting the table. "Go and wash your hands, boys!" she called from the kitchen. "We'll be eating in a few minutes. Then you can tell us what you've been up to."

Thanks to the sea air, they were ravenous so there was no delay in getting ready to start eating. Grandpa Angus kept chickens and so it was omelettes for supper. There were lots of fresh, brown eggs that needed using up.

"Tomorrow," said Edward's mum, "you can both give me a hand to bring some shopping up from the village; we can't live on eggs all the time."

"We mustn't be late back," said Edward, "because Mr McIver's taking us round the lighthouse straight after lunch."

Mrs Cuthbertson smiled. "Don't you worry about that. We won't need much so we won't be long. There's an excellent vegetable garden round the back and Jessie next door has handed in some home-baking and a jar of heather honey from her own bees, so we certainly won't starve."

The rest of the day was mostly spent getting organised. Grandpa Angus helped Jean to put up a camp bed in the room where Edward slept. James was quite happy with the folding bed, but Edward said that he should be the one to sleep in it as James was a guest. He said he'd feel much better if James had the proper bed. James, however, insisted that he would be fine on the camp bed so, in the end, after much to-ing and fro-ing, they tossed a coin! James won and chose the folding bed, which was what he'd really wanted all along! He reckoned that it would feel a bit like camping – and he liked camping.

Everyone slept well and at breakfast the next morning they all enjoyed some of Grandpa Angus's famous porridge, followed by buttered toast with heather honey from Jessie's bees. Edward's grandfather agreed to do the washing-up so that the others could head off into the village to collect some rations. Lunch had to be a very quick affair and a bit earlier than usual as Edward and James were keen to head off to the lighthouse.

When the time came, Donald McIver was waiting for them at his gate. His cottage, the last in the line, was called 'Lighthouse Cottage', which made it very clear where the keeper could be found. Donald McIver was a kindly man. He was not quite as tall as Edward's grandfather and was a little younger, with a mop of bright ginger hair that meant you could spot him a mile away. He was wearing his kilt, especially for the occasion.

"Right, lads!" he called against the wind that was blowing off the sea. "Keep close to me as we take the cliff path. We don't want to get too near the edge. It's a bit crumbly in places. The light is at the highest point on the headland, which is where you would expect a lighthouse to be, I suppose. There are lots of other lights in the harbour nowadays on buoys but, in days gone by, this was the only beacon for miles. There are plenty of jagged rocks around the headland so the lighthouse was always very important. In my book, it still is. Every night, I make sure the light is lit, whatever the weather. Anyway, the tourists love it. I make a bit on guided tours, especially in the summer, but I won't be charging you two. It's free for friends!"

The two boys kept close to their guide as they climbed the well-worn but uneven path that led to the lighthouse. Neither one of them dared to go near to the edge of the cliffs as they climbed higher and the red and white lighthouse grew closer and closer and larger and larger. As they reached the headland, the wind was cold, blustering and fresh from the sea. Despite that, they could hear the constant pounding of the waves against the rocks far below them. The tide was in, completely covering the shingle at the foot of the cliffs, and, high above them, the seagulls were in full cry!

The stone staircase, spiralling upwards to the gallery, was winding, steep and narrow. The boys had never experienced anything quite like it before. Donald

McIver, sensing their apprehension, sent them up ahead of him.

"I"ll be right behind you all the way and I'm nice and fat," he reassured them, "so, if anyone falls back down, they'll be sure of a soft landing."

No one fell. No one needed a soft landing! Once up high on the gallery, Edward and James agreed that it had been well worth the climb. Despite the swirling gulls, they could see for miles. Donald McIver had brought his binoculars and passed them to Edward, who was standing next to him. "You have a good look first and then pass them on to young James here," he suggested. "You'll be amazed how far you can see." He stepped to one side out of the way.

"Hold on a minute!" cried Donald. "There's a ferry just coming in. I think it may be *The Kittiwake* this afternoon. If I'm right, it'll be my young nephew, Alasdair, who'll be in charge. He was made a skipper only last year. You'll easily be able to pick him out. He's got a red carrot top, just like mine." He laughed. "You may even be able to make out some of the passengers. Lots of visitors come to Seal at this time of the year. You can give them a wave, if you like, and see if any of them wave back."

Edward looped the leather strap around his neck and turned the heavy binoculars towards the sea and in the general direction of the incoming vessel. It took a moment or two to set the focus just right and manoeuvre the field glasses into a comfortable position. Just as Mr McIver had said, he could clearly see the ferry as it approached the landing stage. He could even make out several passengers gathered on the deck. They were obviously preparing to disembark. However, just as he was about to wave, he froze.

"What can you see?" asked James and Donald together, but there was no reply. When Edward turned to face them, he was ashen. Without a single word, he tore the binoculars from around his neck and thrust them into Donald McIver's outstretched hands. Then, without any explanation, he set off down the winding staircase at top speed.

James hesitated for only a moment before following in Edward's wake. Perhaps he didn't like being so high up. Perhaps he felt sick. Perhaps he'd seen something that was scary but, as he'd turned to run, Edward hadn't looked scared. He'd looked absolutely terrified!

Spinning round the curving spiral of the staircase made James feel dizzy. On the way up, they'd taken their time; now, headlong, at breakneck speed, it was all he could do to keep his feet. It felt as if the walls were closing in. Trying to keep to the widest part of the stone steps took all his concentration.

"Edward!" he shouted. "Edward! Edward! Stop!" However, Edward was too far ahead of him to hear. Anyway, Edward wasn't listening – and Edward could run!

Once outside, James could see that Edward was a long way in front of him and heading down the cliff path towards Harbour Cottage. He gave chase but he knew that it was hopeless, that he would never catch up. Edward was too quick for him at the best of times. "Watch out,

Edward!" he shouted as loudly as he could. "You're too close to the edge. Keep back! Keep to the path!" It was no good. The wind from the sea swallowed up his words and, in any case, Edward was now far too far ahead to hear him.

The ground was uneven, rough in places, and James struggled to keep his footing. Up ahead, he saw Edward stumble over something in his path. He was too far away to see what it was that had made him lose his footing. All he could do was watch in horror as, with his arms flailing in a desperate attempt to keep his balance, Edward stumbled and fell, disappearing from view over the ragged edge of the cliff.

In sheer terror, James ventured as close to the edge as he dared, threw himself flat on the ground and peered downwards. About fifteen feet below him, well out of his reach, he could see Edward, his stricken face turned up towards him, his hands clinging desperately to a bare root that projected from the cliff face. As James watched, the root came adrift and Edward plummeted downwards towards the angry waves and the jagged rocks far below.

James closed his eyes. He heard no cry. There was only the sound of the gulls and the buffeting of the wind. When he dared to open his eyes once again, he saw that, by some miracle, Edward had landed on a narrow ledge of rock that jutted out from the grey face of the cliff. He was lying very still but, as James watched, Edward slowly got to his feet and pressed himself flat against the cliff, his face turned away from the sea.

"Keep still!" shouted James as loudly as he could against the wind. "Keep still! Don't look down! I'm going to get help! Keep still! I'll be back with Grandpa Angus!"

Somehow, despite the fact that his legs had turned to jelly, James managed to find the strength to run to Harbour Cottage. He'd hardly blurted out the fact that Edward had fallen before Jean began to race towards the headland, followed by Angus, who, on his way out, seized the coil of climbing rope that always hung by the front door. James raced to catch up; they would need him to guide them to the exact spot where, if his luck still held, Edward would be waiting, with his eyes closed and his hands holding desperately to anything he could find that might anchor him to the face of the rock.

James overtook the others and led them up the slope, keeping well away from the sheer drop to his left. He could see Donald McIver hobbling down the hill towards them. Moving at speed, despite his years, Edward's grandfather followed James to the spot where Edward now clung desperately to the bare rock.

Below him, Edward could hear the crashing of the waves. Around him, the gulls screamed a constant warning and, above him, his frantic mother covered her face with her hands and sank to her knees.

Donald McIver had arrived just before them and was lying flat on the ground, talking to Edward all the while. "Stay still, laddie," he was calling down to the petrified boy. "We'll get you up in no time. Angus is here. Just keep still! Try to keep calm! Keep as close to the rock as you can!"

Grandpa Angus peered over the edge and began to uncoil the rope as fast as he could. Carefully, as he'd done many times in his life before, he fastened it tightly around his body and clipped it securely in place.

"Now, you'll need to be the anchor, Donald," he instructed. "Jean, you and James will need to help. I'll send the boy up first and then you must send the rope back down for me as fast as you can. I'll be a lot heavier than Edward, so you'll need to work hard and pull together. Mind you keep well back from the edge!"

"Stop! Angus! Come back from the edge! You're too old for this now and you know that as well as I do. Give the rope to me! You and Donald get ready to take the strain. Jean and James'll have to help when you're bringing me back up." It was Fergal.

Chapter 9

A Rescue

He'd borrowed the ferry captain's binoculars as they'd approached landfall. He should never have left the island. He knew that now. Probably, he'd always known it. He and Jean had been happy there and Edward would have been happy there too, if only he'd been given the chance. As a father, he'd got it wrong. He knew that for sure. All he wanted was to be able to put things right. He owed it to Jean, to Edward and to himself.

To begin with, he'd focussed on the hills. They were old friends. Their familiar outlines seemed to welcome him home.

His own parents, long dead, had never shown much interest in him when he was growing up, but Angus had taken him under his wing from an early age and taught him all he knew about the island. Angus had lived there all his life and he'd taught him all about the hills and the valleys, all about the people and their music and their tales of long ago. In the end, he'd been more than happy to welcome him into his home as his son-in-law.

Angus, a member of the Hill and Mountain Rescue Team, had taken Fergal with him on some of the more difficult climbs and, in time, Fergal had also become a member of the group. He and Angus had helped several walkers and climbers who'd got themselves into trouble on Sutherland Hill. They'd even assisted with some mainland search and rescues in the dead of winter. Fergal, like Angus, had turned out to be a natural climber, just as they were both natural musicians.

Angus was a piper and also played the fiddle with skill, despite the fact that he'd had very little by way of tuition. Fergal had assumed that Edward, like his father and his grandfather before him, would be a musician, but Edward was his own person and Fergal had not allowed for that. Like everyone else, Edward had his own interests, his own strengths and his own failings.

Edward, apart from showing no inclination to become a musician, was also afraid of heights and so, much to Fergal's disappointment, had shown no interest in following in his father's footsteps in any way. He'd been disappointed, so much so that he'd made his own son's life miserable. In the end, out of desperation, Edward had run away from home. No, he hadn't run away from home. He'd run away from him! Jean had told him to let Edward be himself, but he hadn't listened. He'd bullied his own son.

As the ferry had approached the harbour, he'd wondered what he could say to show that he was sorry, to show that he genuinely wanted to make amends. It wasn't going to be easy. His son was afraid of him. No wonder!

He'd turned his gaze towards the lighthouse on the headland, focussing on the gallery and the enormous light. He'd been wondering if Donald McIver still looked after it or if he was getting too old now for all those winding stairs. Much to his surprise, he'd realised that there were three people on the gallery; one of them was looking out to sea. It was only when he saw the boy flying along the clifftop that he realised that he was looking at his own son. Edward might not be a climber – but he could certainly run!

Before the ferry had docked, Fergal had jumped clear, abandoned what luggage he had and raced up the cliff path. He'd watched helplessly as the boy had lost his footing. He'd seen him clinging to the face of the rock before plunging towards the ledge below. Miraculously, it had broken his fall and given him a slim chance of survival, but the obvious danger was that it might not be strong enough to hold the boy's weight for long. Edward desperately needed help and time was short.

Angus had passed the rope to him without a word of protest, helped him over the edge and shouted to let him know that he was ready to take the strain. He, Donald and Jean had braced themselves, slowly letting out the rope as Fergal had begun his descent.

Now it was all up to him.

The descent was slow as the unstable face of the cliff was liable to crumble and send loose stones down towards

Edward. Inch by inch, Angus and the others let out the rope and, inch by inch, Fergal made his perilous journey downwards, trying not to disturb the face of the rock or make any sudden movement that would cause Edward to slip. As he grew closer to his son, Fergal began to talk to him. He thought his voice sounded as if it belonged to someone else.

"Keep very still, Edward. It's going to be all right. Donald, Mum and Grandpa Angus have got hold of the other end of the rope. I'm coming to get you." There was no response. All he could hear was the wind, the churning foam far below them and the screaming of the gulls high above.

Finally, he was able to find a footing on the ledge. It was long and narrow, sloping downwards for at least a hundred yards towards the sea, stopping short about forty feet above the rocks, growing narrower and more slippery the further it descended. For a boy, it was a precarious perch; for a grown man, it offered little room for manoeuvre.

At first, Fergal struggled to find a solid place on which to steady himself so that he could free himself from the rope, all the while reassuring Edward that everything was going to be all right. He knew that Angus and Jean, even with help from old Donald, would not be strong enough to bear the weight of both himself and Edward so he would have to take his chances. The most important thing was to rescue his son.

"Keep still, absolutely still," he whispered. "Don't make any sudden movements. Don't move at all until I tell you. I'm going to fasten this rope round you and then Mum, Donald and Grandpa Angus are going to pull you up. Keep calm and do exactly as I tell you." Edward said nothing. Frozen with fear, he only just managed to open his eyes. Listening intently to his father's instructions, he suddenly began to shake from head to foot, making it almost impossible on the narrow ledge for Fergus to loosen the rope from his own body and transfer it to Edward's smaller frame. Somehow, he managed it.

While Fergal worked to secure the rope, Edward's eyes never left his father's face. He seemed to be trying to say something but, if any sound emerged from his trembling lips, it was carried off on the wind. Finally, it was time to make the journey back up the face of the cliff.

"When you're clear of this ledge and well above my head, use your feet to push yourself clear of the rock. That'll keep you from getting hurt as you go back up. When you get to the very top, Grandpa Angus will take the rope off you and send it back down for me. Do you understand?" Edward nodded.

Fergal lifted his eyes towards the edge of the cliff high above him. "Pull!" he shouted. Gradually, holding grimly to the rope, Edward began to rise. As Fergal watched, his son slowly travelled up the rock wall, swaying a little as he did so until, finally, he disappeared over the edge. There was a loud cheer from a group of onlookers who had obviously gathered on the cliff path. The welcome sound drifted down on the sea air and told Fergal that all was well. Edward was safe.

Edward's feet making contact with the cliff had sent fragments of rock hurtling downwards towards his father's anxious, upturned face. Fergal just managed to protect his eyes with his hands, but this slight movement was almost enough to send him plunging backwards into the sea far below. Struggling to keep his balance, he somehow managed to steady himself just in time to seize the rope that Angus had sent back down as swiftly as he could.

"Ready!" Fergal braced himself. "Pull!" He felt the rope tighten and then, half climbing, half pushing against the rock, he began his ascent. Far above him, the rescue party now had some additional help in the form of three hikers, who'd seen what was happening and had raced up from the ferry. They were now adding their considerable pulling power to make the job a whole lot easier. There was another loud cheer when Edward's dad finally appeared, safe and sound, over the top of the cliff, and the assembled team could congratulate each other on a job well done.

Angus put his arm around his son-in-law. "Well done, laddie," he whispered in Fergal's ear. "You got here just in time. You did a grand job."

Fergal nodded. It was all he could manage. After he'd got his breath back, he checked on Edward, who was still in shock, trembling from head to foot and unable to speak. As the anxious group, including James, gathered round him, Jessie, Angus's next door neighbour, came hurrying up the hill carrying a heavy blanket over her arm.

"Stand back, now. Let Jessie see to him," said Angus. "She's the district nurse around here. She'll check the lad over better than we could."

After wrapping the blanket round the shivering boy, Jessie quickly checked to see if he'd suffered any obvious injuries.

"He's going to be fine," she reassured everyone within earshot. "Amazingly, he only has a few scrapes from the rock. Apart from that, I think he just needs time to get over the shock. We all do! We need to get him home and into bed with a hot water bottle. He's shivery. Once we've got him safely back, I'll ring for Dr Graham to come and have a look at him. I've a telephone in my cottage so it won't take a minute. Best to be on the safe side." She turned towards Edward. "Are you able to walk, Edward?" There was no reply. Edward just stared ahead of him as if he'd lost the power of speech.

"What about you?" Jessie turned to Fergal. "You're a brave man and just as lucky as your son here, by the looks of things. Are you hurt?"

Fergal shook his head. "No bones broken, Jessie. I'm fine, thanks," he answered. "I'm very grateful to you for all your help and you're quite right; it would be a good idea to check things over with the doctor, if you don't mind giving him a ring."

Jessie hurried off to make the call while everyone else began to go their separate ways. Angus thanked the hikers, who'd even brought Fergal's haversack up the hill from the ferry, and his friend and neighbour, Donald McIver, for all their help with the rescue, while Fergal carried his son back towards the cottage and a warm bed.

Jean lingered for a moment to have a word with James.

"Thank you, James. It was your quick thinking that helped save the day. I will never be able to thank you enough for what you did. You really are a true friend."

Leaving him to walk back down the hill with Edward's grandfather, she hurried after her husband, who was almost at the front door of Harbour Cottage by the time she caught up with him. James watched as they all went inside.

Grandpa Angus and James walked slowly down the slope. The sun shone. The wind blew. The gulls cried. It was as if nothing had happened. They walked in silence until they reached the very end of the row of cottages.

"It doesn't seem real," said James. "It's like it never happened, as if I'd dreamed it, like a nightmare."

"I know exactly what you mean," replied Angus. "One minute it's a nice, peaceful, sunny afternoon and the next… " He didn't bother to finish his sentence. "Come on, James. We'll take a wander round the back and have a sit down in the garden for a while. I think we'd better leave the others to sort themselves out, don't you?" James agreed. It was beginning to dawn on him how near they had come to disaster. When he looked down at his hands, he saw that they were shaking.

At the end of the garden was a wooden table with four chairs around it. Angus and James made themselves comfortable in two of the wicker chairs, but it was quite a while before anyone said anything. Finally, it was Angus who broke the silence.

"Jean was right. You did a really good job today, James. Edward is very fortunate to have such a good friend."

"I didn't do much at all," replied James. "I tried to stop him but he's such a good runner. I just couldn't catch up with him and I didn't even know why he was running.

One minute, Edward was looking through the binoculars and the next he was off down the stairs and running for his life. I shouted after him, but I don't think he could even hear me. He just kept going."

Angus looked thoughtful. "Donald said that Edward had the binoculars trained on the ferry so he must have seen his father on the deck and taken fright. He'd given him the slip, hadn't he? He would know that Fergal would not be too pleased about that so he'd be trying to get back to the cottage as fast as he could. Must've been that. He'd be trying to get back to warn us, afraid of his father's temper."

James didn't know what to say. He just nodded.

Angus looked serious. "Edward's dad, like the best of folks, has his faults but he's also got his good points. He's had some knocks in his life and, from what Jean's been telling me, that's changed him. When he lived here on Seal, he was a different man altogether. Anyway, I'm hoping he's come to put things right with his family, especially with Edward. All he needs is to be given a chance – but that'll be up to Edward and Jean."

"Are you two all right?" It was Jessie calling from her own garden next door. "I've called Dr Graham and he's on his way over right now. He'll give Edward, Fergal and your Jean the once over and maybe give them all something to help them to sleep tonight. It's the shock that can cause problems later on, you know, but don't you worry because they're going to be absolutely fine. I'm sure of it."

Angus smiled. "Many thanks, Jessie," he called. "We're fine. The two of us are just sitting here recovering. It's been quite an afternoon and your help was very much appreciated. You came along at just the right moment!"

Jessie smiled. "A bit like Fergal," she said. "Thank goodness he came along in time and thank goodness he has a head for heights. Anyway, I doubt your enormous feet would have fitted on that narrow ledge, Angus!"

They all laughed and felt a bit better. Jessie continued, "I'm just about to go up to the hives to tell the bees all about it. When anything happens, I always tell the bees. They like to be kept informed about everything that happens on the island." James looked unconvinced.

"Oh yes, Jessie's right," agreed Angus. "Births, deaths, weddings, christenings, the bees always have to be told. It's a custom that's been observed around these parts for generations." He winked at James. Then, turning back to Jessie, he called out, "Would you like a couple of visitors next door? I don't expect James has seen beehives up close."

James wasn't sure that he really wanted to be up close to large swarms of bees but, as he was reassured that it would be quite safe, he allowed himself, accompanied by Grandpa Angus, to be led up the garden path towards the far end of the next door cottage garden. Jessie led the way, her overall flying in the breeze, her cheeks flushed with the unexpected events of the afternoon. She was keeping a professional eye on Angus and James, who, like the rest of the family, looked as if they needed a bit of tender loving care.

"Come on, you two!" she called over her shoulder. "We mustn't keep the bees waiting."

To his surprise, James enjoyed his visit to the beehives; it put some distance between himself and what had gone before. While he and Edward's grandfather looked on from a few yards away, Jessie, now dressed in her protective veil, talked softly to her bees as they carried on with their work. Some were busy in the lavender beds on either side of the path, while others seemed to have travelled further afield, drifting to and fro from the banks of heather on the wild moorland immediately behind the row of cottages. The scented air was heavy with the constant droning of the bees.

"Many thanks, Jessie," said Grandpa Angus. "You've done your duty by the bees and they've helped us all to recover from the day's adventures. Now that we've got our breath back, James and I had better head off down to the post office for a quick check on how Hamish is managing on his own. I left him to it today. We're leaving the family alone for a bit. They've a lot to talk about."

The post office was not far away, on the main street and close to the ferry terminal, so it took no time at all to get there. When they arrived, Hamish, Angus's cousin, was sitting on a high stool behind the counter drinking a cup of strong, black tea. He looked pleased to see them. "Now then, Angus," he called out from behind the post office grill, "I'm hearing there's been a bit of a fuss up at the headland. I take it everybody's safe and sound?"

Grandpa Angus nodded. "Aye! Fergal arrived at just the right moment so he got the lad up in no time. Mind, it was a close run thing and it could easily have gone the other way. They're all up at the cottage now. We're leaving them to sort themselves out." He turned to introduce James. "This is James, Edward's best friend from the mainland. He raised the alarm and helped save the day. No question about it."

Hamish beamed. "Well done, James! Edward's got good taste in friends, I think!"

While the two men talked together, James took the opportunity to have a look around. In some ways, the post office reminded him of home because the shop was in two distinct parts, with one half being used as a post office and the other as a sort of general store.

As Grandpa Angus and Hamish were now deep in conversation about the business of the day, he wandered round the section that was the general store. There were all manner of things that tourists might like: post cards, fishing nets, beachballs, sunglasses and lots of tartan souvenirs. On one shelf, he couldn't help noticing a display of fancy jars of heather honey. He guessed that it had probably been made by Jessie's bees.

"Right, James," Grandpa Angus finally called from the doorway, "I think we can probably head for home now and organise something to eat for everybody. It'll probably be down to you and me so I hope you can cook." James had never cooked anything in his life before, so he didn't feel particularly confident.

As they were leaving, Hamish called after them. "Do you think the family'll be coming back to live on the island again, Angus? It would be good news if they did. We could do with some youngsters. Too many old fogeys around these days."

Angus paused in the doorway. "Old fogeys, indeed! Speak for yourself, Hamish! As for your question, well, we'll have to wait and see. I don't think Fergal's ever been happy since they moved to the mainland all those years ago, and I'm pretty sure that Jean would be more than happy to come home again but, as I say, we'll just have to wait and see what happens. It's up to them and, after all, they've got Edward to consider. They'll want to do what's right for him. Still, Edward loves the island so I don't think he'd take much persuading!"

James felt his heart sink. It sank even further when Hamish followed them to the door. "Angus, tell them that if they want a nice cottage there's one on my land that could do with a tenant, and I could also do with a hand on the farm these days. That new ram that came on the ferry's a right handful. I think I'm getting a bit too long in the tooth for the likes of him these days!"

As they walked back up the hill, Edward's grandfather turned to James. It was as if he'd read his mind. "Don't you worry, James. If they do decide to come back here to live, you'll always be welcome to come and visit. You'll not lose your best friend. Don't you worry about that."

"Do you think they will come to live here on the island?" asked James. He tried not to show how anxious he was feeling but his face gave him away.

"I don't really know," answered Grandpa Angus. "It would be nice for me. It would be good to have their company and also, although they don't know it yet, I'm writing a book about the island and I would love to have Jean and Edward help me with the illustrations. They can draw and paint. I can't! However, as I said to Hamish back there, we'll have to wait and see. The decision is theirs to make." He smiled at James.

"My daughter and Fergal were at school together here, you know. They've known each other all their lives but, when Edward came along, they moved to the mainland. They didn't want him to have to make a trip on the ferry every day just to get to and from school. It was what they'd had to do because there is no high school on the island. There's a wee school for the kiddies but all the older ones have to travel to the mainland to the academy in Castle Bay There and back every day, no matter what the weather! It can be a bit rough in the winter."

As they approached Harbour Cottage, James fell silent. Edward was safe. That was the most important thing. He hoped that things were going to be all right with his mum and dad and he could see that Seal Island would be a great place to live. It would be wonderful for Edward. In fact, it would be just fine for everybody. Well, not quite everybody. He couldn't help thinking that, in a few weeks time, he might very well be walking through the gates of Craigallen High School all on his own.

Chapter 10
People and Plans

Edward looked at the clock. Twenty-past-six. Too soon to be thinking about getting out of bed, far too soon to be getting up, but he knew for sure that he wouldn't be doing any more sleeping. He was wide awake. James, in the folding camp bed next to the window, was still fast asleep, hidden from view under the blankets.

Outside, the sun was up. The early morning light flickering through the curtains told him that it must be windy on the moor; the shadows of the racing clouds played against the blind as they swept across the heath behind the row of cottages. Soon, Seal Island would be waking up, bustling with local people and tourists all going about the business of the day. Soon, the ferry would be preparing for its first trip, heading for the mainland and Castle Bay.

When Edward thought about all that had happened, he felt cold, despite the weight of the eiderdown that his mother had added to the enormous pile of woollen blankets already on his bed. He knew that he would always remember the day he'd fallen from the cliff, that he would always remember the deafening cries of the gulls and the pounding of the angry waves far below him. Most of all, he would always remember how his father had risked his own life in order to rescue him and how he'd kept him safe from harm.

The last person he'd expected to see, when he'd looked through those binoculars, was his own father standing on the deck of the ferry, his haversack by his side, his sights firmly set on Seal Island. All he'd expected to see on the deck was a boatload of birdwatchers and maybe another sheep or two, but there he was, his own father, looking straight at him. Clear as day! At that moment, running was all that came to mind. The need to reach his mother, his grandfather and the sanctuary of Harbour Cottage had driven him on. He'd run to be safe and, instead of that, he'd simply put himself and others in terrible danger. Edward shut his eyes tightly and pulled the bedcovers up to his chin, but it was no good. He was wide awake now and the pictures in his head just wouldn't go away.

Talking with his mum and dad had been difficult at first but, in the end, it had been the right thing to do. His dad had said how sorry he was that he'd made life miserable, not just for Edward, but for the whole family. He'd said that he was sorry for how he'd behaved, that he knew he'd made everyone unhappy, that, more than anything, he was sorry for making Edward feel bad about himself. He'd taken the blame for everything that had gone wrong and simply asked his family for the chance to put things right. Once he'd realised where Edward had gone, he'd known at once that he needed to follow him, needed to come to the island just to find out if there was any way that he could make amends. Edward and his mum had listened in silence and then they'd told him how brave he'd been that day, not just on the face of the cliff but in being brave enough to say that he'd been wrong and that he was sorry.

Edward had also said that he was sorry, sorry that he couldn't play the piano, sorry that he'd been a disappointment and sorry that he'd run away. He'd given back the money he'd taken from his dad's secret hoard. Not much had been spent. His dad had just laughed and said that he'd have to use some of it to pay for a new pair of jeans as he'd snagged his best ones on the the cliff. Edward's mum had pointed out that, if she simply repaired the trousers, there would be enough money left to buy some new drawing things for Edward and herself. Fergal had handed the bag of money over to Jean and sat with a tartan rug over his knees while the necessary repairs were carried out. He'd told Edward that, with luck, there might still be enough money left to buy the new bicycle he'd been hoping for. There would be no more waiting to pass music exams, no more arguments and, most important of all, no more trips to The Lockie School of Music.

"You're not a disappointment," his father had told him, while he was waiting for Jean to finish her sewing. "You were pushed into something that wasn't right for you."

He'd looked straight at Edward. "This is all down to me," he'd said. "You are you. There are lots of things that you are good at and I haven't always appreciated that." He'd looked around the comfortable, cosy sitting room of Harbour Cottage, with its white plaster walls, grey stone fireplace and ancient furniture – and he'd smiled. "I'm glad you came back here, Edward. I've always felt at home in this place in a way that I have never felt at home anywhere else. Leaving the island was a big mistake. I know that now – and I think your mum agrees with me. We were happy here."

Edward thought about what it might be like to live here on Seal Island. He'd been to the island several times to visit Grandpa Angus but staying here for good was quite a different matter. His mum had agreed that moving back to Seal was an idea worth considering and, on the whole, Edward agreed with that. He loved Seal Island and he especially liked the thought of having more time to spend with Grandpa Angus. He felt sure they could all be happy here but, deep inside, there was a nagging ache that wouldn't go away.

He'd been friends with James for a very long time – forever, really! They'd been all through school together, right from the beginning, and moving on to Craigallen High was something they'd been looking forward to for ages. Now, it looked as if that wasn't going to happen. Even though he wouldn't know anyone there, he'd have to go to Castle Bay by ferry every day and James would move on to Craigallen without him. He didn't want to think about it. Thinking about it made him feel empty and cold.

"Are you awake, Edward? What time is it? Is it time to get up?"

James's voice took him by surprise.

"Sh!" came the immediate response. "No! It's just after seven, so everyone will still be in bed. I thought you were asleep. I've been awake for ages. Did you sleep OK?"

James sat up. His hair was standing on end. "Not really," he whispered. "I kept thinking about yesterday. It wouldn't go out of my head. I kept looking to see if you were all right. Are you?"

Edward had to think for a moment. "Yes, I think so," he replied. "To be honest, I was just thinking how it would be if we came to live on the island. Things may turn out that way and it would be good to see Grandpa Angus more often, but it would be horrible travelling to the mainland by ferry every day, especially in the winter, just to get to school. I'm pretty sure that I'd be sea-sick all the way. Mum and Dad used to live here when they were young and they had to travel to Castle Bay High every day. Mum said she hated the winters when the seas could be rough and they had to set off in the dark. I think she's worried about that bit, worried for me. It wouldn't be like going to Craigallen."

In the silence that followed, James looked at Edward and he couldn't help thinking that he looked just as miserable as he felt. However, during the night, when he hadn't been able to sleep, he'd been doing a great deal of thinking. Now, sitting up, he ran his fingers through his wild mop of hair and turned towards Edward. "I've been thinking about Craigallen too," he said. "I've been thinking about how awful it would be to start there all on my own in August. We've talked about it all year, talked about all the things that we were going to do, made plans about the football club and everything!"

Edward looked close to tears.

James decided to take the bull by the horns. "Edward," he whispered, still aware that they were probably the only ones in the house who were awake, "I think I might have a plan. I don't know if it would work but do you want to hear it anyway?"

Edward emerged from under the eiderdown. "Yes," he replied. "I definitely do!"

By the time the rest of the house was awake and breakfast was on the kitchen table, the plan was approved and ready to go but, for now, only Edward and James could know about it. They were agreed that it could work, but a great deal depended on what happened in the next day or two. First of all, they had to take a trip to the harbour and that red telephone box by the jetty. James had some coins that his mum had given him before he'd left home so that he could ring her if he felt homesick. He didn't feel homesick at all, but he did want to talk to his mum and dad, and he needed to do that before they came to collect him, which would be all too soon. There was no time to lose.

"Mum, is it OK if James and I head down to the village for a while?" asked Edward. "There's a lot of the island that James hasn't seen yet. Also, he promised his mum that he'd give her a ring. We could go to the telephone box on our way."

Jean looked at Angus and Fergal before answering. "I don't see why not," she replied. "However, we would need a firm promise from both of you that you will keep well away from the cliff path! We've had quite enough excitement for one trip." Both boys were more than happy to confirm that they would be keeping well away from the cliff path and danger of any kind. As they left, Edward's mum called after them. "Tell Sadie and Rab that we're looking forward to seeing them tomorrow."

Mr and Mrs McLintock were already in the shop and preparing for a busy day when the phone rang. "It's James!" Sadie McLintock called to her husband. "No, he's not in any trouble. He sounds fine but he wants to talk to both of us about something so can you come through to the back for a minute, please? Apparently, it's very important."

Rab McLintock locked the front door of the shop while he went through to the back shop to listen in. "I'm here!" he shouted so that James could hear him. "Is there a problem?" He and Mrs McLintock listened with their ears pressed close to the receiver. From time to time, they could hear coins clinking in the callbox as James had to keep putting more money into the slot. They listened intently and, in the end, they understood. Exchanging glances, they nodded to each other before telling James that they thought his plan sounded very promising but, obviously, they would have to wait until they'd talked with Edward's mum and dad. "See you all tomorrow!" they managed to shout – just before James ran out of coins!

Three people were now queuing outside the phone box so the boys made a hasty exit and headed for the beach. There was nothing more to be done. Everything depended on the mums and dads now. All that was left was to enjoy

Seal Island and hope that things would go according to plan.

"We're on the wrong side of the island to spot any seals," explained Edward, who'd visited the colony with his grandfather, "but we may be able to find some fossils." They climbed over the harbour wall and made their way along the shingle. No luck! No fossils to be seen today! There were lots of shells and pebbles of all colours, but no fossils, not this time. Still, with luck, there would be lots of other opportunities to search for them.

They were on their return journey along the beach, walking towards the ferry terminal, when they heard Grandpa Angus calling from the jetty. "Come on, you two! We're all going to The Woodrush Hotel for lunch – fish and chips! Any good?"

Lunch was very good indeed. "Fresh fish, all caught this morning!" the waiter had informed them as he'd taken their order. "You won't find any better anywhere." It all lived up to expectations so very little was left at the end of the meal. Nevertheless, everyone agreed that they could still manage some strawberries and ice-cream.

"I'm hearing from Jean that your mum and dad have arranged to come over for a day or two," said Grandpa Angus. "They'll be very comfortable here. It's the best hotel on the island. It used to be the only one, but these days we get lots more visitors, even big cruise ships, so two new ones have opened up not far away. However, this one is still the one I would choose."

The afternoon began with a trip to the post office to collect a set of keys from Hamish. This was a complete surprise to Edward. "Where are we going?" he asked, as they headed away from the seafront and towards the hills.

"You'll see soon enough," replied his mum.

It only took about ten minutes to reach their destination. "This is Hillcrest Farm," announced Edward's grandfather, pointing to the large sign by the main gate. "It's where Hamish lives. I think he's hoping that he's found some tenants for the old shepherd's cottage he's hoping to rent out."

Edward's mum pulled a face. "I don't know about this, Dad," she said. "If we do come to live on the island, we'll want somewhere decent. 'Old Shepherd's Cottage' sounds as if it could be a bit run-down and smelly. I couldn't be doing with that."

Grandpa Angus had the keys and so he was the one who opened the front door, but then he stepped back so that Jean could be the first person to cross the threshold. For a moment, there was silence and then, as everyone else tentatively followed her inside, she found her voice. "Wow!" was all she could manage at first. "I didn't expect this!" she cried. "What's been happening here?"

Grandpa Angus looked pleased with her reaction. "I didn't say anything," he boomed. "I wanted you to see it for yourself. Well, what do you think?"

Jean struggled to find the words. In the end, she just said, "I love it!"

The cottage was much larger than expected and freshly painted and decorated; the windows were sparkling clean and it was obvious that a brand new kitchen had been fitted. Grandpa Angus explained that Hamish, eager to attract the right sort of tenant, had taken advice from Jessie, Grandpa Angus's neighbour, who had an eye for what was right on the home decorating front. "They've been working on it for months," continued Edward's grandfather. "Jessie's got a keen eye for this sort of thing and, just between us, I'm beginning to suspect that she's got a keen eye for Hamish as well, although I don't think he's realised that yet!" Edward's grandfather tapped the side of his nose and winked, knowingly. Everybody laughed!

Outside, the garden was mainly laid to grass, with plenty of room to have whatever you wanted. Fergal was impressed. "You could have fruit trees, vegetables, chickens, and even a shed."

It was clear that the cottage had made a very good impression on everyone and Edward could see that it was a lot better than where they lived in Craigbank. "Well, Edward? What's the verdict?" asked his dad. "You're the one who led us here in the first place, so what do you say to coming here for good? Would you like to live here on Seal Island?"

There was a pause. James kept quiet and stepped back. Everyone waited in silence. Finally, Edward spoke. "Yes, I would like to live here – and I think this is a good house." That was what everyone wanted him to say, so he said it, and some of it he actually meant. Mainly, he didn't want to be responsible for any more disappointment.

"But?" asked his mum. "I think there might be a 'but'."

Edward looked at James. "It's just… " Then he looked down at the floor. He couldn't find the right words. In the end, he just shrugged his shoulders and smiled a pale sort of wobbly smile that faded very quickly.

Edward's mum and dad exchanged glances. It was his mum who finally broke the ice. "I think we get it," she said. "You're thinking about James and how you'd looked forward to being at high school together and how you don't really want to be travelling to Castle Bay every day in winter to a school where you don't know anybody and where nobody knows you. Am I on the right track?"

Edward, his face now an unconcealed mask of misery, just nodded. For the second time that day, James could see that he was close to tears.

Jean put her arm round Edward's shoulders. "As it happens, Edward, your dad and I have been giving that problem a great deal of serious thought and you may be surprised to know that we have come up with a plan, a plan that might even work, but we can't say any more about it until tomorrow. We need to have a talk with James's mum and dad. We'll have to see what Sadie and Rab have to say about it!"

Edward and James looked at each other. It seemed as if they were not the only ones who'd been having ideas. Grandpa Angus gave them one of his reassuring winks and a knowing smile. Behind his back, James crossed his fingers for luck!

Many miles away on the mainland, Sadie and Rab McLintock were locking up earlier than usual, making sure that everything was in perfect order. Two old friends had agreed to look after the shop for them while they were away; they were always happy to step in when required.

"It'll be good to see the island and Angus again, even if it's only for a couple of days," said Sadie, thinking aloud. "We haven't been to Seal for years so I'm really looking forward to tomorrow. We'll need to be off bright and early to catch the ferry. Let's hope we get a smooth crossing."

Her husband nodded in agreement. "The weather forecast is good so don't worry about the crossing. We'll be fine. I was just thinking that we haven't been back there since our birdwatching days. That was ages ago. We ought to have taken James across long before now. It's a great place. I bet he's loving every minute of it."

"I do hope that the boys' plan meets with approval," said Sadie, checking one more time to make sure that the shelves were tidy and the cash register safely locked up for the night. "I don't see any reason for it not to work, and James and Edward are pinning all their hopes on it, but it all depends on Jean and Fergal. We'll have to wait and see what they think when we see them tomorrow."

"I'll be surprised if they don't approve of it," replied Rab. "Mind you," he added, turning the enormous key in the front door lock and making doubly sure that the two large, metal bolts were rammed firmly into place, "there is also the matter of *our* little plan. Let's not forget about *our* plan!"

Sadie hung up her apron on its hook next to the back door. "Oh yes!" she called over her shoulder, as she turned to make her way upstairs. "There is *our* plan. I haven't forgotten about that. Oh no! Not for one minute! How could I? I wonder what the others are going to think about it. Still, we'll soon find out!"

As he followed his wife upstairs, Rab McLintock was feeling optimistic. He had a good feeling that everything was going to work out for the best but, like James, all those miles away on Seal Island, he put his right hand behind his back and crossed his fingers – just for luck! Best to be on the safe side!

Chapter 11

Rosemary and Others

Whenever Rosemary thought about the staircase, she felt warm inside. She knew that she would always remember it, even if she lived to be a hundred years old. Every step took her closer to Miss Gilpin and the enormous grand piano that almost filled the upstairs salon. However, she would have to remember that Miss Gilpin was now Mrs McIntosh. Mr Lockie had changed his mind about women having to give up their work when they got married. Rosemary had performed a dance of celebration in the downstairs hallway when Mrs Lockie had told her the news.

"A lot of nonsense!" Mrs Lockie had said firmly. "We won't be having any more of that!"

Rosemary was pretty sure that Mrs Lockie had had quite a bit to do with the sudden change of mind on her husband's part. That was confirmed when Mrs Lockie joined in with the dancing. She'd held hands with Rosemary and skipped up and down the hallway until they couldn't dance any more for laughing.

Almost as soon as she rang the bell, Mrs Lockie was there to open the door for her. "Hello, Rosemary, my dear," she said. "It's lovely to see you. How are you getting on?" She always said the same things and always with the same welcoming smile that made Rosemary smile back.

"Very well, thank you, Mrs Lockie," she replied. She always said that, while wiping her outdoor shoes several times on the doormat just inside the front door.

As Rosemary disappeared round the first bend in the staircase, Mrs Lockie watched her go and lingered for a few moments. Nowadays, there was a new routine to be followed. She always stood listening at the foot of the stairs until she was quite sure that the pupil in question had reached his or her destination, before she made her way back down to the kitchen in the basement. In the end, Edward had been found and he'd come to no harm, but she'd never forgotten that frantic search that had failed to find any trace of a boy who'd been entrusted to the care of The Lockie School of Music. She was quietly determined that never again would she or Mr Lockie have to explain to a distressed and angry father that his child was missing!

The door to the basement was left ajar so that she would hear the bell whenever a pupil arrived and had to be let in. Lately, she'd begun to think she was getting a little hard of hearing. Not ideal for the wife of a music teacher! She'd have to start wearing the hearing aids that had been prescribed for her several months before. All she had to do was remember where she'd put them. She hoped she hadn't thrown them away.

Rosemary almost ran up the steps with her music case in her hand. On the first floor, she bumped into Mr Lockie, who was collecting some sheet music from the cupboard next to his own room.

"Rosemary! How nice! I believe I'm going to be entertained by you at my wife's forthcoming afternoon tea party. She was telling me all about it last evening. How wonderful! I'm looking forward to that. Miss Gilpin... No! Sorry! I really do need to get this right. *Mrs McIntosh* tells me that you're doing very well indeed."

Rosemary felt her cheeks turning pink. "I'll be playing 'Romance' by Beethoven," she whispered. "It's one of my examination pieces."

Mr Lockie seemed to approve. "One of my own personal favourites," he said. Mr Lockie smelled of cigar smoke and Rosemary rather liked the smell of cigars. Sometimes, he smelled of whisky. She didn't mind that either. It reminded her of her grandfather, who enjoyed a glass or two in the evenings when he'd finished working in his garden and washed up after supper.

On the next floor, she paused to listen just outside the door of the main salon. She could hear that one of the older pupils was struggling with a very difficult piece. It sounded tricky. Some kind of dance, she thought. A polka maybe? One day, she hoped that she would be able to play really difficult music. Perhaps, one day, she'd be able to play almost as well as Mrs McIntosh and teach other people to play the piano. She was undecided. She was also seriously considering being a deep-sea diver.

As she reached the very top step, Rosemary thought of Edward. They'd often met here at this point on the stairs. He'd always looked so sad. She'd tried smiling at him, but he hadn't smiled back, not as if he actually meant it anyway. She remembered how miserable he'd been at the concert when all the mums and dads had come along. He'd hated every minute of it and she'd felt sorry for him.

Every week, she'd questioned Mrs McIntosh about Edward but there hadn't been any more news, not since he'd run away. Mrs Lockie had been able to reassure everyone that he was safe. Edward's mother had written a letter to Mr Lockie to say that Edward had been found and that he was very sorry for running off and causing so much trouble. Thankfully, Mrs Cuthbertson had also said that she and Edward's father did not blame anyone else but themselves for what had happened. Everyone at The Lockie School of Music had breathed a sigh of relief. Edward's mum had also said that she would be in touch with them again once things had settled down. That had intrigued everyone, especially Rosemary!

"Come in, Rosemary!" called the new Mrs McIntosh, when she heard the sound of eager footsteps on the landing. "I've been looking forward to your arrival even more than usual. You'll be pleased to know that I have some very important news for you. Some extremely good news, in fact."

"Is it about Edward?" asked Rosemary.

Mrs McIntosh adjusted the piano stool to the correct height for her pupil and then, while Rosemary was making herself comfortable, she took a long, blue envelope out of her handbag and held it up in the air like a trophy.

"You've been asking me every week if I had any more news about Edward. Well, finally, there is lots and lots of news! Look at this!" she announced. "It's a letter from Edward's mother. She wrote to thank all of us for the help we'd given Edward and to apologise once again for any trouble that had been caused. Poor Edward! They eventually found him on Seal Island, where his grandfather lives. Poor boy! He'd hated music lessons so much that he'd actually run away from home. I've never known a pupil go to such lengths before."

Rosemary couldn't understand how anyone could fail to enjoy music lessons, but she didn't say so. She just concentrated as hard as she could on what Mrs McIntosh was saying. As she sat and listened, the story began to unfold. Apparently, Edward and his family had now moved to live on Seal Island. Mrs McIntosh explained roughly where it was. "It's an interesting place just off the west coast," she said. "I once went there to see the seals and visit the seagull colony. I'd like to go back some time." Rosemary liked the idea of going to see the seals, but she wasn't quite so sure about the gull colony. It was probably a very noisy place and, in her limited experience of seagulls, they could be messy.

Mrs McIntosh returned to the letter in her hand and began to read out loud:

'Like all of us, Edward loves Seal Island, but school was going to be a problem. Travelling to and from the mainland by ferry every day in the winter was not something that had a great deal of appeal. In addition, Edward and his friend, James, had been looking forward to starting secondary school together in Craigbank. Because of this, and unknown to us, the two boys hatched a plan, not knowing that we'd had the very same idea. For it to work, however, James's parents also had to be in favour of it. Happily, they were all for it.'

Mrs McIntosh looked up to make sure that Rosemary was following. She was.

She read on:

'During term time, Edward will stay with James's family in Craigbank so that he and James can still go to the same school together. During the school holidays, things will almost work the other way round so that James, Edward's best friend, will be able to come and stay with us here on the island. There's lots to do here so it should work out just fine for everyone. We thought you'd like to know how it all turned out.'

Mrs McIntosh turned to the second page of the letter, which went on to explain that James's parents had surprised everyone. They'd come up with a plan of their own. Remembering holidays that they'd all enjoyed on Seal Island, they'd decided to rent a cottage there so that, on occasion, during term time, they could take James and Edward over for short visits and then, during the long summer holidays, James's family would be able to return to Seal to do some climbing and birdwatching, while the boys went fossil hunting or doing whatever it was that they wanted to do.

"It sounds as if Edward's escape to Seal Island has had a huge effect on lots of people," said Mrs McIntosh. "It's amazing that things have worked out as well as they have and thank goodness for that!"

The letter was carefully folded once again and returned to its envelope. It was obvious that Rosemary wanted to know more, but the clock on the mantel was a reminder that the lesson needed to begin. "The main thing is that Edward is safe," said Mrs McIntosh. "We can talk about it again at break time so keep all your questions until then, Rosemary. For now, we'd better make a start. It won't be long until Mrs Lockie's tea party, so we'd better polish up your pieces for the big day. Lots of mums and dads will be coming."

"And grandfathers!" added Rosemary, as she opened her music case. "Grandfathers are very important people."

"Indeed they are!" agreed Mrs McIntosh. "Don't worry. Parents *and* grandparents will be most welcome. There will be quite a few grans and grandpas with us on the big day. In fact, it wouldn't be the same without them."

Rosemary took the sheet music from her case and set it on the stand, wriggling on the stool to make quite sure that her feet could reach the pedals. She settled her hands on the keys of the giant piano and began to play. Her teacher leaned back in her chair and listened. She watched as the tiny fingers travelled effortlessly over the keys and made them sing. The music rose and fell in the comforting stillness of the room, before floating gently through the open window and down into the garden far below. The beech tree, now autumn brown and heavy with nuts, rustled in the faintest hint of a breeze so that a single golden leaf broke free and floated, just like the melody itself, higher and higher on the warm afternoon air, before drifting downwards to find its final resting place in Mapledene Avenue.

In the garden of number 152, Bob Harkins put down his broom and checked his watch. He'd had enough of sweeping up leaves for one day. Leaning on the front gate, he thought he could hear music, but he wasn't sure if it was coming from the music school across the way; he wondered if he'd left the wireless on. The avenue was quieter than usual and the breeze was travelling in his direction, so he supposed it could be someone playing in one of the upstairs rooms. The windows would be open.

Yes, it was piano music, a piece that he thought he'd heard before. It sounded familiar. Alas, a motor-bike came roaring along the avenue, sending the fallen leaves flying high into the air. The engine noise drowned out any other sounds, annoying everyone within earshot, especially Bob! Still, soon it would be time for tea, but there was an errand that needed doing before that.

Closing the gate behind him, Bob slowly crossed over to the other side of Mapledene Avenue and made his way towards the front door of number 145. He couldn't hear the piano any more; someone must have closed the window. Ringing the front door bell, he waited for a few moments before rattling the knocker. He'd noticed lately that Marjory was a bit hard of hearing so he thought he'd better make a bit of extra noise, like that infernal lad on the motor bike! Once she was down in the basement, it could take a while before Mrs Lockie answered the door.

"Oh, it's you, Bob, making all that noise!" exclaimed Mrs Lockie. "I might have known it. How are you?"

Bob apologised. "Sorry, Marjory. I thought you might be downstairs," he explained, laughing. "I was making sure of a quick response!" He picked up some post that was lying on the doormat and handed it over. "Postie must've been a bit late today," he said as he gave it to Mrs Lockie. "He usually stops for a bit of a chat, but I must have missed him this afternoon."

Mrs Lockie placed the bundle of mail on the table next to the hallstand. She couldn't help noticing that there was a postcard on top of the pile. It had a picture of a harbour on the front, a harbour with an enormous seagull standing guard on a grey stone wall.

"Mostly bills, I expect," she said, pulling a face. "They're nearly always bills these days."

Bob leaned against the fence. "By the way, have you heard anything more about that young lad that ran away? Edward, wasn't it?" asked Bob. "I've been wondering about him quite a bit recently. Any news?"

Mrs Lockie smiled. "Bob, I'm so glad you've asked me about that. We've been waiting for news and it finally came this week. We've had a long letter from his mother, telling us all about what's been happening. Of course, the main thing is that Edward is safe."

"Yes indeed," said Bob. "I did hear that he'd been found. Still, I've been feeling a bit guilty about it all. I sent his father the wrong way, you know! I shouldn't have done it, but the man just rubbed me up the wrong way, so I sent him off in the opposite direction. Irresponsible! I know! Just couldn't help myself." He tried not to notice the stern look of disapproval that was now aimed in his direction.

Mrs Lockie continued with her story. "Poor Edward! He was never going to fall in love with the piano. It just wasn't for him. His father knows that now. I suspect he always knew it. Anyway, the boy had finally had enough and so he ran off to join his grandfather on Seal Island. Gave his father the slip and made his own way there. In the end, the family thought he'd actually had a sensible idea and now they're all going to live there. What do you think of that?"

Bob shook his head in disbelief. "I never would have thought it," he said. "It's a long way to Seal Island. Not bad going for a young lad to organise all by himself. Must be a bright boy."

Marjory Lockie agreed. "That he is!" she said. "He doesn't appear to be musical but he's bright enough in other ways. Apparently, he's going to be staying with friends on the mainland during school time to avoid the ferry, especially in winter."

Bob nodded his approval. "Much better than travelling on one of those ramshackle ferries in the winter," he added. "Seal Island's a great place but a bit wild when the weather turns rough. I used to go there with the camera club."

"Oh, I'd forgotten about that," said Marjory. "I'd forgotten about your artistic talent with the camera. It seems that Edward is also talented in that direction. It turns out that his mum is something of an artist and he seems to have inherited her skills. She says in her letter that she and Edward are going to help her father, who's writing a book about the island. They're going to do the pictures. Isn't that wonderful?"

Bob nodded once again and then, avoiding Mrs Lockie's disapproving gaze, he made a further confession. "You know, Marjory, I watched him run off that day. I saw him heading along this avenue as if his tail were on fire. I even watched him help himself to a bike from outside the school over there. I really should've shouted or done something – but I didn't. Anyway, I'm glad now that I kept out of it as it all seems to have worked out for the best, except, of course, for the rather unfortunate owner of that bicycle."

"Oh! I hadn't put two and two together. I hadn't realised that Edward had been the mystery thief," said Mrs Lockie. "However, I did mean to tell you about that stolen bike. Everybody's been keeping an eye out for it. Apparently, the postman found it right outside the art gallery. It was sitting in full view in the parking ground. He recognised it from the notice on the school gate and took it back a few weeks ago. The caretaker took it straight round to the boy's house so there was a happy ending after all. I like happy endings. Don't you?" Bob agreed that he did prefer happy endings to any other kind.

At that moment, an eager face appeared around the door. "Grandad!" Rosemary cried. "I've got lots to tell you! Remember Edward, who ran away, well– "

"Hold your horses!" cried Bob. "Mrs Lockie, here, has been telling me some of the story so we can share what we know while we're having tea!"

Mrs Lockie patted Rosemary's shoulder. "I've been telling your grandfather a little bit about Edward's adventures, but I'm sure you have lots more news for him. I gave Mrs Cuthbertson's letter to Mrs McIntosh, and I imagine she's been reading it to you."

Rosemary said that the very long letter had been read; not a word had been missed. However, quite suddenly, she looked rather solemn. "I'm glad that Edward is OK," she said. "He always looked sad when I met him on the stairs. I'm afraid he didn't like playing the piano. In fact, I'm pretty sure that he hated it."

"Never mind, dear," replied Mrs Lockie. "We can't win them all."

As Rosemary and her grandfather reached the gate of number 145, Mapledene Avenue, they unexpectedly had to turn back. Mrs Lockie was calling after them and following them down the path.

"Wait!" she called. "I must tell you! This postcard, which has just arrived, is from Edward. Can you believe it? We were just talking about him and… you really won't believe this… he's having music lessons, after all. He's written to tell us that his grandfather is teaching him to play the bagpipes and he's enjoying every minute of it. He has finally found a way to make his own music!"

Rosemary cheered and, holding her music case with one hand and picking up the hem of her skirt with the other, she performed her own version of the highland fling right there on the pavement!

At that moment, they were interrupted. Christina, a tall girl with long, fair hair tied up in bunches, arrived for her piano lesson, so Mrs Lockie had to hurry back indoors. As she watched Christina climbing the stairs, she told herself that, all in all, it had been a very satisfactory day. Different – but very satisfactory!

Downstairs once again, she pinned Edward's postcard to the kitchen notice board so that Mr Lockie would see it when he joined her at the end of the day's lessons. She placed it right in the centre so that the picture would catch his eye straight away. On a grey sea wall, a friendly seagull stood on sentry duty.

Before starting to make the evening meal, Mrs Lockie allowed herself a few minutes in the armchair by the window. From there, she could look out over the garden towards the beech tree and the orchard beyond. There was more land behind the terrace than most people realised; beyond the orchard, the ground slipped away towards the river, where she often liked to sit under the willow and watch the wildfowl that passed that way. Sometimes, there was a heron and once she'd even seen a family of otters. Unusual sights in the heart of the city.

To reach the riverbank, she had to pass through her rose garden and past the vegetable patch. She thought she'd probably get up early the next morning to wander down there for a while. There were always jobs to do and then, of course, there was the shed!

Right next to her, just outside the window, was her herb garden. She thought she might take a walk outside to see if she could find some fresh parsley. Salad tonight! Too warm for cooking! Still, tomorrow morning she would bake some bread and the kitchen would smell wonderful all day and then, in the afternoon, there might be time to spend in the shed, her very own shed!

Mrs Lockie looked around her kitchen. It was vast. At the far end was a large, stone fireplace. In summer, she liked to put a vase of flowers in the centre of the hearth. In the spring and summer there were always plenty to choose from and, now that it was September, the bright colours of the chrysanthemums burnished the garden with red and orange and gold. People said that she had 'green fingers'.

When they were first married, Mr Lockie had tried, in vain, to teach her to play the piano. It had proved to be hopeless, but the fingers that had consistently failed to find the right notes could make just about anything grow. They could make their own kind of music!

The kitchen shelves were already laden with golden jars of pickles and jewel jars of jam; fruit cakes and home-made biscuits were stored away, ready and waiting for the day of the party tea. Not long now! The nimble fingers that failed at the keyboard could work their own magic in other ways.

Mrs Lockie's gaze kept returning to the notice board and Edward's postcard. How she sympathised with him! "You're quite right, Edward!" she said out loud to the empty room. "You're absolutely right! We all have to make our own music." Rising from her chair, she picked up the hem of her skirt and, rather like Rosemary, performed her own brief version of the highland fling. Through the open kitchen window, she pretended that she could hear the distant sound of the pipes.

Tomorrow afternoon, it being Saturday, a day when there would be no pupils to be listened for, no pupils to be let in and no stair carpet to be vacuumed, she would make her weekly trip to the bottom of the garden and the wooden shed that was tucked well out of sight, beyond the rose garden. This was her shed, her very own refuge. Painted green, its diamond-paned windows were trimmed with bright yellow curtains and its window boxes were packed full of pink geraniums. It was her own place, the place where she kept her gardening tools, her plant pots and, best of all, her drum kit!

In another kitchen, a double-decker bus ride from where Mrs Lockie now sat, James and Edward were busy at the kitchen table, finishing the weekend's homework. Always best to get it done straight away so that Saturday and Sunday would be free!

James was finishing some Geometry that required a great deal of concentration and careful measuring with a ruler and protractor, while Edward had just packed away his Maths books and was looking at the timetable for the week ahead. On Monday morning, there would be English first thing and the class had been asked to prepare some ideas for an essay. They'd been given the title, which was to be: 'A Walk in Autumn'. To his own surprise, Edward found himself thinking about the beech tree.

Now that it was September, Mapledene Avenue would be thick with fallen leaves. He remembered how he'd kicked his way through them as his feet had trailed in the direction of The Lockie School of Music. The tree would be at its best, heavy now with golden leaves. Once, he'd watched two grey squirrels hunting for nuts in its branches and once, during break, he and Miss Gilpin had spotted seven of their young ones playing 'hide-and-seek' around the trunk, ducking and diving so fast that it was impossible to keep track of them.

He was glad that he'd sent that postcard. Nowadays, when he thought about Mapledene Avenue, it didn't seem quite as bad. Even the staircase, although he was glad not to have to make his way up those steps ever again, didn't seem as ominous as once it had and, if he shut his eyes, he could almost smell the lavender polish, the trail of cigar smoke on the landing and the faintest hint of whisky in the air.

Still, it was all in the past now. In a few days, it would be half-term and time for them all to take their first trip back to Seal Island. He was looking forward to it and he knew that James was, too. He was looking forward to seeing his mum and his dad again. They were now happily settled in the shepherd's cottage and his dad was managing the farm for Hamish, although he was still finding time for his music and often played for the tourists in the hotel by the harbour. His mum and Grandpa Angus were both busy working on their book, *A Year on Seal Island*, and Edward was hoping to do some drawings of birds for it when the holidays came round. It felt as if the pieces of a giant jigsaw were finally falling into place.

"Clear the table, please, boys!" came the call from downstairs. It interrupted Edward's thoughts and made James drop his ruler as he measured out his final angle. It was Mrs McLintock. "We're shutting up the shop in five minutes so it will soon be time to fetch the fish and chips. Time to set the table!" No one needed to be told twice!